THE MARRIED MAN

A Story of Love, Betrayal and Forgiveness

Diane M. Waterman

A Lovely Lullaby

It sounded like the voices of angels singing at a distance as Wyatt lay down his head for the night. He knew there was a pub in the community. It had to be coming from there. He was staying at his friend's cabin for the weekend which was very close to the community of Acklin. He hummed along to the song knowing the words well. *Will The Circle Be Unbroken* was a song that brought warm memories of his mom singing.

Melody came to his thoughts and pulled at his heart strings as it did every night when he remembered her and longed for her. He suddenly felt warm all over, like someone had just laid a warm blanket to cover him as he drifted off to sleep.

Other Books by Diane Available Online

When Lilacs Bloom (2013)
You Have To Go Now (2017)

The Married Man

Copyright © 2020 by Diane M. Waterman

dianemwaterman@hotmail.com

All rights reserved. No part of this book may be used or reproduced by any means, graphic, electronic, or mechanical, including photocopying, recording, taping or by any information storage retrieval system without the written permission of the author except in the case of brief quotations embodied in critical articles and reviews.

Cover Design by Mariana Coello
 Interior Formatting: Edge of Water Designs, edgeofwater.com

ISBNs:
Paperback 978-1-77374-070-6
Ebook 978-1-77374-071-3

For the love that was lost, the love that was
found and the love that is everlasting.

Diane

*There is a reason we meet everyone in life. Sometimes it is
simply to inspire us to write a novel. The things we can't
have here on earth we can always have in a book.
Then again, anything is possible if we simply believe.*

This is a fiction that was sparked by a true story.

CONTENTS

Chapter 1: Happy Birthday 1

Chapter 2: Seriously? 10

Chapter 3: Wyatt's Regret 13

Chapter 4: Brief Interlude 15

Chapter 5: There is Hope 17

Chapter 6: Wyatt's Truth 30

Chapter 7: Puss n Boots 34

Chapter 8: Naughty Pictures 37

Chapter 9: Matter of Time 42

Chapter 10: The Truth is Unveiled 45

Chapter 11: Begging Forgiveness 54

Chapter 12: Complete Madness 60

Chapter 13: Going Out With Grace 66

Chapter 14: Face To Face 71

Chapter 15: Jenny 76

Chapter 16: Gone Fishin' 79

Chapter 17: Song From the Heart 92

Chapter 18: A Dad's Healing Love 95

Chapter 19: The Watch Rep 102

Chapter 20: The Final Call 105

Chapter 21: The Final Email 108

Chapter 22: Five Years Later 112

Chapter 23: Free At Last 118

Chapter 24: Final Goodbye 121

Chapter 25: Melody Turns Fifty 127

Chapter 26: Surprise, Surprise 132

Chapter 27: Wyatt's Promise 140

Chapter 28: The Porch Swing 143

Chapter 29: Where's Wyatt 149

Chapter 30: Grizzly Adams 154

Chapter 31: Big Decision 158

Chapter 32: And Then There Were Two 161

Chapter 33: Count Their Blessings 166

Chapter 34: The Intruder 175

Chapter 35: Forgiveness 184

Chapter 36: Graduation Day 190

Chapter 37: The Ultimate Heartbreak 196

Chapter 38: Picking Up The Pieces 200

Chapter 39: Midnight Swim 206

Chapter 40: Going Home 211

About me 219

Chapter 1

HAPPY BIRTHDAY

It was the end of September 2003, Melody's favourite month of the year in the town of Glendale, Alberta. The population was fifty thousand plus, so it was regarded informally by many as a small city.

Melody turned 35 today. It was her birthday. She was very proud of the fact that she had saved enough money over the past ten years to open her own shop. It was small but it had her name on it. This was huge for her! Melody's Jewellers had officially opened one year ago and she was already making a nice profit. Her father always told her she had a good head on her shoulders and she believed him. It had given her the courage and confidence she needed in her life to always push herself to work hard, and all the hard work had finally paid off.

Melody had worked in the jewelry business since her first part time job while still in high school at the age of seventeen. Although her first love was music, the jewelry business gave her joy as well. Finding that perfect gift that put a smile on her client's faces made her feel good inside. She enjoyed the excitement of being a small part of other people's weddings, birthdays, anniversaries or 'just because' celebrations. Whatever the occasion that made people happy, she was happy to be a part of.

Melody decided to walk to work today and take in all the fall colors that dripped from the huge maple trees that were nestled close together down every lane. The leaves were showing off their fall colors of yellow, orange and crimson. They were flickering in the sunlight. It was delightful to watch. She breathed in the cool air with each step she took. It felt wonderful and made her feel light and happy. It was just that kind of day! You couldn't have wiped the smile off her face if you tried.

It wasn't long before her mind wandered. As much as she practiced living in the moment she didn't stay there for long. She was an over thinker. Her mind soon drifted off like it always did on her walks. She went back to all she had survived in the past few years and to where she was today. She was proud of herself and how she didn't give up on life when it would have been so easy to do so. She was a fighter!

Melody's two sisters and mother had died in a car crash three years ago and she thought of them and missed them daily. She had spent many days when she could hardly get out of bed because of it. The tragedy had torn her and her father's whole world apart. They struggled their way through it together. They went to grief counselling together and stuck with the program for as long as it took to give them both some kind of healing and peace. Now when she thought of her missing pieces, she thought of them with a smile on her face and not on the floor bawling like she had been for many months after the crash. The ache of missing them was always in her heart. She accepted that would never leave but she and her dad had made a pact that they would go on to live their lives to the fullest. Losing their family made them realize just how short life could be. Her dad had picked her up many times when she fell apart as she did for him. It was a bond now that kept them close and only they understood. Every time she thought of her dad she had a smile on her face. He was precious to her.

As for men in her life, Melody had one serious relationship in her adult life that had lasted 10 years. Her ex-boyfriend Michael was a man who couldn't commit so they had ended their relationship. She also knew she had pushed Michael even further away when her sisters and mom died. She had admitted to Michael that her grief had caused some of their issues of the distance between them in the end. She had known heartbreak of the worse kind with Michael too but when she thought about him now it no longer hurt. She had been stripped to the core at a time when she was already so vulnerable. So many times she needed Michael's arms around her but he only became colder during her time of grief. It made her resent him. She had forgiven him since then. She had learned that much in her grief counselling sessions. Resentment can ruin your life and affect everyone around you daily. She didn't want to be that person who hangs on to anger. It was freeing to forgive him and herself and move on.

Melody thought she would never get over the heartbreak in the beginning. Even though she loved Michael, she did always feel he was not the love of her life, whatever that was? She was yet to meet this person who could sweep her off her feet. She had promised herself she would never love again, at least not until she found what everyone wrote about in all the romance novels she had read. Yes, she was a hopeless romantic and a dreamer at heart. She wrote many poems and songs throughout the years and many were about that perfect love. She had not experienced it yet but she was definitely a believer in true love.

A wedding seemed far-fetched to her but it was something she had always dreamed of and still came to her mind on days like today. Her birthday was always a reminder for her that time was flying by quickly. Having children was something she longed for as well but was not something she had planned for, and now she feared it might be too late at her age. The clock was ticking and her friends reminded her of it all the time. She had already accepted that if it was meant to be it would be, if not she would have to live with it.

Melody glanced down at her watch and it was 9:30 already. She had enjoyed the walk very much and felt energized by the time she arrived at the mall. She quickly unlocked the door to her little store and went inside.

She rushed around the store doing her usual routine before she would have to open the doors to the mall at 10 am. Her co-worker Bridgette was going to be late today because she had an early dental appointment. It was a Friday pay week so Melody hoped it would be a busy day. "I better hurry and open the safe," she muttered as she made her way to the office in the back of the store. She turned the dial until she heard the fourth click. She gripped the cold handle and pulled the heavy door open. Melody removed each container with care that held the precious trays of diamond jewelry. She carried them to the front of the store, carefully placing each tray inside their designated showcase. When she finished she walked around to the front of the showcase to make sure everything looked tidy. She locked each showcase before unlocking the sliding doors and pushing them back to their hidden compartments to open the store to the public.

Melody bent down to pick up a piece of paper off the floor and as she came back up she covered her mouth to stifle a yawn. "I saw that." said a voice from behind her. She turned to look and saw there was a man walking by with a grin on his face. She laughed and he stopped in his tracks, came back and stood directly in front of her on the outside of the showcase.

"How are you?" he asked.

"Good thanks, you?"

"I'm fine." My God he was handsome! He was tall, slender and was wearing a white t-shirt underneath a faded jean jacket. His blue jeans fit him perfectly. He was well manicured and looked similar to her favourite movie star Richard Gere. Same hair and brown, squinty eyes…

"Kill me now!" she whispered under her breath.

"What was that?" he asked.

"Nothing." she replied with a smile.

"I'm Wyatt Walker." he said as he reached out his hand.

"I'm Melody, Mel Newman." she stammered as she reached to briefly shake his hand. She pulled back quickly because the electricity she felt from the touch was off the charts. She was sure he could see she lit up like a Christmas tree at the sight of him.

Melody and Wyatt chatted for about ten minutes. They quickly found out they knew a few people in common. Wyatt worked with people that she sang with sometimes. He was an operator at one of the big oil companies and a part time helicopter pilot. "Flying is my passion though." he said.

"That's very cool." she replied trying to be cool herself while the butterflies were dancing around in her belly like dragons.

"Do you like to fly?" he asked still smiling.

"It is not my favourite thing to do but I do it when I need to. I have never been in a helicopter, seems a little scary to me."

"Not at all. It is very safe."

"I'll take your word for it. My stomach flips just thinking about it. It's my birthday today!" she beamed; not knowing why in the heck she felt compelled to tell him that.

"Oh, Happy Birthday. How old? Or should I ask? I hear its rude." he chuckled.

"No, it's fine. I'm 35. Thank you."

"Nice, we are the same age."

Melody was daydreaming already and she needed to give her head a shake to snap out of it. The last thing she wanted this man to know was that she was drooling inside. She had never felt this kind of electricity before with a man and it was throwing her off her guard. It was exciting, yet scary as heck that he was stirring something up inside her! The wall Melody had kept up to keep her heart safe always worked but in this moment she suddenly felt it slowly sliding to the floor. She was pretty sure men she had met could feel that wall from her. It kept them at a safe distance. Even though it was three years since Michael, she turned down anyone who asked her out, not wanting to ever hurt like that again. Besides, she had not met anyone that intrigued her enough to even think about it, until now. There was never the connection with Michael that she was feeling in this moment with Wyatt. She couldn't imagine what it would be like to have to let someone like this go. It was best she didn't even go there.

"I better get to work. Nice meeting you." she said as she turned to walk away. As she stepped forward she tripped on one of the empty containers she had left on the floor after putting the diamonds out. Her hand went out and she caught the glass counter top just in time to stop herself from falling. Wyatt reached out to grab her hand and said, "Whoa, be careful there." She felt heat in her face right away from the embarrassment.

"I'm fine!" she snapped. Melody pulled her hand away sharply, ticked at herself for being so silly and clumsy! He was grinning again. She could see he was almost fighting a full blown laugh. "Cripes sake!" she muttered. She suddenly had the urge to slap that smile right off his face! Yep, now he knew he made her nervous. She wondered if she made him nervous too. If only she could read his mind. She definitely saw lust in those squinty eyes but he acted cool, unlike her.

Wyatt could see Melody was a little nervous and that made her even more attractive to him. She was breathtaking! She made him nervous too but he hid it well. She was beautiful with her slender body and her full breasts that showed just a touch of cleavage under her form fitting, knee length, midnight blue dress. She wore a black cropped, dress jacket over it. Classy, was the first word that came to mind when he first looked at her. She was sexy too with those sling back heels, even though they weren't too high because she was already tall, must be 5'9 he guessed by his 6'1 stature. Her long dark hair looked soft to touch. She had deep, grey eyes that drew him in like a school boy wanting his first kiss.

He could see a lot of wisdom in them for a young woman. What struck him the most was her sweetness. He could tell right away she had a heart of gold. He had to give his head a shake and keep moving. "It was nice to meet you too. Enjoy the rest of your day." He waved and walked away. What he wasn't prepared for was that this woman would not leave his mind that easily.

Bridgette breezed by Melody and said, "Sorry again I'm late Mel, Happy Birthday!"

"Thank you. It is okay, it's not getting busy yet. I managed getting everything out on time. What's this?" she asked. Bridgette was carrying an armful of flowers in one arm and a cake from a bakery in the other.

"I lied." Bridgette confessed. "I didn't have an appointment. I wanted to pick these things up for your birthday. You deserve this and more." She passed the bundle of daisies to Melody and laid the cake on the counter for her to look at.

"Awe, it's beautiful and I love daisies! Thank you so much Bridge, you didn't have to." she said as she hugged her tight.

"You're welcome Mel. By the way, who was that guy you were talking to?" Bridgette asked while taking her coat off as she went around the corner to hang it up in the office.

"Just a man who stopped to say hi." Melody replied. She felt herself blush a little.

"Mmmhmm. He is handsome."

"You think so?"

"Yes, I do think so!"

Melody smiled as she leaned in to smell the daisies.

Chapter 2

SERIOUSLY?

Melody could hear Levi scuffing his feet at a distance, as she did every morning around this time. Levi was a homeless man that pulled at her heartstrings every time she saw him. She looked out and waved to him and he gave her his toothless smile and waved back. "Good morning Levi," she called out. "Morning." he mouthed back to her. She knew he could never remember her name no matter how many times she told him and that was okay. He was a sweetheart and always put a smile on her face to start her day.

It was 9:45 am. Melody cleaned the glass showcases and then placed the cash drawer in the till. Bridgette was carefully placing the diamond trays in the showcases. "Take your time Bridgette. I will vacuum this morning." Both of them worked away until it was time to open the doors.

Two days had passed since Melody met Wyatt. He was on her

mind constantly, so much so it was annoying her. She was cleaning the watch counters when suddenly she looked up and there he was again. Their eyes locked and suddenly the world went away! "Morning Melody," he said as he smiled with that twinkle in his eyes.

"Oh, hello again." Her heart was racing and her hands started to sweat.

"Can I get your phone number please?" Something Melody never did was giving out her personal number to anyone. She had to think about it for all of two seconds.

"Sure." She grabbed her business card, turned it over and jotted her number on the back. When she passed the card to him she couldn't help but notice he was wearing a blue, plaid flannel shirt under his jacket with a white t-shirt peeking out under the collar. She imagined herself kissing the crook of his neck. When she realized what she was thinking her eyes snapped shut! She passed him the card and he put it in his coat pocket. Her hands were trembling a little. She quickly put them to her side!

"Thank you," he said. "Are you okay?"

"Yes, I'm fine!" she replied with a nervous smile. She was irritated with her foolishness. Why was she acting this way?

"Well, I am married but I like you a lot."

Melody could feel her eyes widen and her face go red with anger. "I'm not interested!" she snapped.

"Alright, sorry." he said and he turned and walked out.

"What just happened?" Bridgette asked when she saw Melody turn so red.

"You don't want to know!" Melody exclaimed as she rolled

her eyes and grabbed the cleaning cloth and Windex off the shelf behind her. She nearly rubbed the glass off the countertops with the added pressure of being so angry!

"Who the fuck does he think he is, coming in here and getting me interested and asking for my phone number when he is married? He must be crazy!" she muttered as she worked. She felt like throwing something! What made her the angriest was she actually even felt it may be a 'love at first sight' experience after he was there the first time. It sure felt like what they wrote about in all the books. "What a nerve!" she sputtered. She would put him out of her mind completely now because she had thought about him for two fucking days straight. "Jerk!"

She looked around to make sure no one else was near who might hear her rant. Yes, she could have a potty mouth if someone made her angry. She could go off like a mad woman! Not something she was proud of but it made her feel better in the moment. Sometimes she wondered if it was a weakness or strength. It was a part of who she was that she kept under control most days. Michael loved it about her and said it turned him on when she got mad at him. He thought she was hilarious. That would set her off even more. She certainly didn't feel funny at the moment!

Chapter 3

WYATT'S REGRET

Wyatt brought the axe down hard on the chunk of birch. You could hear the crack in the air. There was more than cutting up fire wood that was on his mind. For weeks he kicked himself for being a jackass and falling for a woman while he was still married. It bothered him that he had upset Melody more than anything. He knew she was a sweetheart and didn't deserve such bullshit from any man. He hated that he didn't control himself better.

He was stunned by how attracted he was to her. Even now he couldn't get her off his mind. He should have known better than to treat her that way. He could see she was a class act. He felt terrible! It was even worse to disrespect his wife that way. He knew he was wrong no matter how lonely he was with his wife. No one in his life had drawn him in before like Melody did. The tables had turned the moment he spoke to her. Yes he was married a long time and the fire had gone out in their marriage, still no excuse for his behaviour. He and Trish just went in two different directions in life and had lost touch. Even with marriage counselling they couldn't seem to reconnect. They stayed together for the sake of their son and daughter, so they told each other. Neither of them had the courage to take the next step.

He needed to figure himself out before he could ever be with another woman. He knew a divorce was inevitable but he just wasn't ready. He was second guessing his decision now. What was the chance he would ever meet another woman he would have a spark with like he did with Melody. Each swing he made with the axe was harder than the next. He knew he had to go see her again and apologize and he needed to tell his wife it was time to make a decision about at least separating. It would be hard to do after 12 years and would be hard on their children. Deep down he knew it would be even harder and unfair to have their children live their lives with unhappy parents.

Going to see Melody again was risky. He feared he might melt right there in front of her or she might knock his head off. She looked angry enough to and he couldn't blame her. He had felt the pull right away when they met. How could he feel this much instantly? He couldn't understand it because it was the first time he ever felt anything like it. It scared him and thrilled him at the same time!

Every night when he went to bed all he thought about was Melody and she was the first thing on his mind every morning. He felt like a real jerk for insulting her but she sure woke something up inside him. That he knew for sure!

Chapter 4

BRIEF INTERLUDE

Two months had passed by quickly and Melody, Bridgette and two other staff members Carol and Gabe, were setting up the store for the Christmas season. "Pass me the red bulbs please." Melody asked Gabe, as she stood on the ladder putting the final touches on the Christmas tree. When she was finished she climbed down and went behind the diamond counter humming along to the Christmas carol Silent Night that was playing in the background. She was checking to make sure all the sale price tags were in their right places. Gabe put away the ladder and boxes for her without her even having to ask. "Thank you Gabe." she said.

"No problem." he replied. Melody knew she was sure blessed to have such good staff.

She was leaning into the glass to check the small writing on each tag when she suddenly saw feet on the other side of the showcase. She stood up and looked Wyatt straight in the eyes!

He looked as magnificent as ever, except this time he had a look she never saw before on his usually smiling face and eyes. It was a look of nervousness and maybe sadness. She was certain she had that same look on hers as well. She was long past the anger that she had felt towards him. He was still on her mind at least once a day which irritated her to the core. Now it felt like the world had stood still again. Neither of them could speak, they just stared into each other's eyes. A minute or two passed and then he turned and walked away without a word. Melody stood there frozen!

For the rest of the day her heart felt like it was in a tight ball and the questions rolled around in her mind. The way he left Melody knew she would probably never see him again. As the years went by she thought of him many times and often wondered what had happened to him, and why he came to see her that day.

Chapter 5

THERE IS HOPE

It was January 11, 2013, almost ten years later, and it was a chilly minus 23 outside. Melody was in no mood to go see a psychic and she didn't know why she let Bridgette talk her into it. She wanted to stay bundled up in front of the fireplace. "C'mon Mel, pleeease. Do it for me." Bridgette had begged her over the phone. "I'm tired of seeing you down in the dumps."

"Okay! I'll do it for you but you know I am not interested in meeting any more men. I told you before that I was done with even dating again. I must need my head checked." Melody groaned and rolled her eyes. "Give me time to get up and shower."

"YES!! I'll be there in an hour to pick you up!!" Bridgette replied with a little too much enthusiasm for Melody's liking. She did however appreciate her friends concern for her. Bridgette was happily married and had two beautiful children. She wanted Melody to experience that too. Deep down Melody wanted it too but had accepted it just wasn't in the cards for her. She did believe in mediums and psychics but did not want another man for a long time to come, if ever! The last thing she needed was to find out there might be another one on the way, so to speak. She would humour her friend today and then maybe she would back off for a while. That was the plan.

A year had passed by since Melody and Garrett finalized their divorce. Their marriage had been dead for a year before they both came to an agreement to end the misery they were living in. She had put up with his bad gambling habits way longer than she should have. It was the lies that bothered her the most. He had hid it well for the first year they were together but then she started seeing red flags thinking he was cheating at first, until one day after a big fight he had admitted he was a gambling addict. The casino was where he would disappear to for hours at a time not answering his phone.

It had been four long years and she was tired of fighting with him about it. He broke every promise to her along the way. If he told her the truth from the beginning instead of hiding his issue, she would have never married him. It was hard for her to give up on him because there was chemistry between them but she had had enough. They had enjoyed each other's company for the most part and they loved to go dancing. He was more affectionate and caring than Michael had been. She enjoyed that side of him but over time she started to feel that even his affection was a part of his manipulation. That, and her not wanting to be alone again for a long time, kept her hanging onto him for far too long. She had waited for seven years after her break up with Michael to give anyone else a chance, only to be let down again. She knew she deserved better than to be lied to and manipulated on a regular basis. She learned a lot about addiction and how it affected a person's character and relationships in the time she had been with him.

The other negative thing with Garrett was he didn't like to kiss and he had good reason, he wasn't good at it. As much as Melody tried to change that, they just weren't connected that way. It was a big disconnect that she felt. She yearned to be kissed passionately and wished many times over the years that she had made that a more important factor before she accepted his marriage proposal. It didn't seem to bother him at all that they rarely kissed. She tried everything to fix their issues but it took two, and he was not motivated to even try. He would say he would, but his actions clearly spoke otherwise.

After she found out the truth about his addiction she decided not to have a child with him because he never proved himself to her that he could keep his word. He broke her heart so many times with his lying.

Melody had bought him several watches and rings over the years they were together. Some went missing that he couldn't account for; making up lies that he lost it or someone stole it. She had learned enough over time to know that he probably pawned the jewelry to gamble. She had given him a beautiful heavy gold bracelet that was worth two thousand dollars for the last Christmas they were together. When that went missing she was done!

Now between running her store and singing every second

weekend with her band, she was exhausted most days but at least was happy to be free of the constant drama with Garrett. Melody believed she would never have a child now at 44, besides her life was far too busy.

She had felt like a failure at first in getting divorced and then she turned around the negative thinking and saw all the positives of not wasting her life anymore being unhappy. The hard stuff would pass. Everything passes in time. She was wise enough to know that much.

Melody had finally moved on from him and sweet Bridgette was now trying to set her up already with somebody new.

When they arrived at Phil the psychic's home, it was actually nothing like Melody had expected. It was by a lake half an hour outside of town. When they walked inside she loved the big windows and the lighting. There were great views from every window. "I could live here. It's beautiful." Melody stated.

Phil shook both of their hands with introductions. "Thank you Melody for saying that. I love it here. Please come in and take a seat." Melody suddenly felt a little off. Her stomach was queasy. That was never a good sign. She knew it was nerves about what she was about to be told. Phil asked why they were there.

"We want to know if Mel has anyone new coming into her life in the love department." Bridgette said.

"Not that I want it. Just please don't tell me I am going back to Garrett." Melody said with a tone of displeasure.

"Who's Garrett?" Phil asked.

"My ex-husband. I'm kidding." she chuckled. It was best she

tried to see the humour in all this.

"Well let's hope not. I can't control your future but I can predict it for you. Any of it can change with your own free will. Let me take a look here." Phil had a large deck of cards in his hand. He shuffled them carefully many times and laid 6 of them out on the oak dining room table in front of her.

Melody took a deep breath and waited for Phil to speak. "Well, you definitely won't be with Garrett again but I do see someone new coming within two to four weeks." Melody gasped and her mouth fell open.

"You must be kidding?" Melody asked nervously. Bridgette was smiling like a Cheshire cat. Phil went on to say, there would be an instant attraction with her and this new man.

"Instant attraction?? Great, just what I need, a heart breaker!"

"His hair is like…hmmm… Grizzly Adams."

"Grizzly Adams? I am not fond of long hair on a man. Yes, I admit I do have things that turn me on and off with how a man looks, don't we all?" she asked defensively. She glanced at Bridgette who was giving her the judgemental eye.

"No, it's not long, it's above the ear." Phil stated. "Let me think of a celebrity who has similar hair." Phil paused for a minute. "Rex Tillerson has similar hair. It is a mixed color but more grey."

A cross between *Grizzly Adams* and *Rex Tillerson* hair? Hmmm…The hair seemed to be a big deal in the description. "Having a full head of hair is not so important, but nice." she stated. The more Phil said the more Melody felt herself actually opening up to the idea. "This is crazy!" she mumbled, getting a little cautiously excited about the prospect. She had a lot of different emotions going on that were both confusing and conflicting.

Phil went on to say this man would be mid-forties, he has all his own teeth and he is tall at 6'1. Bridgette giggled at the teeth remark. "I guess having your own teeth is always a good thing." she chuckled.

"He is widowed." Phil said.

"He is young to be widowed." Bridgette stated.

In Melody's mind she just could not imagine falling in love again. It was the last thing she wished for. This man was going to be a widower? That part was the one thing that would stump her later on. Was Phil just telling her this so she would give the guy a chance? That would not be professional. Phil would be so right on with everything else. Her mind was racing! She wasn't expecting this at all. Now what?!

She was told before she met Garrett by a different psychic, that she was going to meet him. The description had been exact but it took two years after the reading before they had actually met. This was only going to be a matter of weeks according to Phil. "I guess we will soon see how accurate Phil was in his predictions." she said to Bridgette as they climbed aboard her SUV.

"Yes we certainly will!" Bridgette replied. She had a brilliant smile on her face like she had just won the lottery.

Two weeks after the reading with Phil, Melody was sitting at home on a Friday evening. It was January 25, 2013. She suddenly had a thought come to her to go back on an online dating site. Right away she pushed the thought away. She had no desire to go back to the craziness of online dating and politely having to say no thank you but best of luck, to a bunch of men and then getting fed up in a couple of weeks and end up taking herself off there. She had done that same routine a dozen times over the years while she was single. It was frustrating to say the least. She also knew people who had met the love of their lives on them, so there was a glimmer of hope that pulled her to keep trying.

"Go back on." The voice whispered, tormenting her.

Melody finally gave into it, believing by now her intuition was speaking to her and she needed to listen to it. "Never know I may meet Grizzly Adams/ Rex Tillerson on there." she mumbled sarcastically.

She went through the same routine of writing a down to earth profile and she posted her usual photos, adding a few recent ones. Before she even had the photos all posted she was receiving messages. She rolled her eyes! "Why do I keep doing this to myself?" she muttered. Melody preferred meeting someone the old fashioned way, face to face, but this was a different time from when she was younger and she knew she had to adjust, like it or not. She had only met with a few men for coffee in all the times she had been on the dating site. They never turned into a second date. There was never a spark for her. Most times she went on this site because like most people who went on them, she was lonely. She was asked out often but was so afraid of being hurt again. Most times the person who asked her out just wasn't for her. She had all kinds of excuses for turning men down.

Melody had replied to about 25 messages within the first

two hours after she went back on. She replied to each person with the same response she normally gave. No thank you, best of luck. None of them pulled her in to write anything more in her responses. She would get the odd one that wouldn't take no for an answer and would keep writing her seven or eight messages sometimes trying to get her to respond again. She ignored them or blocked them if they wouldn't give up. Over the years some would ask her why she didn't want to talk or meet them after she had sent them a friendly no thank you to their request. She would be honest to them in a kind way and say there was just no spark. One man kept persisting and she couldn't block him because he was so sweet and kind. She finally told him the half-truth that she was looking for someone with more in common. He wrote back and thanked her for being honest. She couldn't tell him the whole truth, that he was too old for her. Twenty years was a lot and his picture showed he didn't take good care of himself. She could never hurt his feelings by insulting him in any way about his looks.

The worst day for her on the site was when a man sent her a picture of his penis. Yep! A dic pic! She opened his message and there it was in full view. You could say she was shocked! His caption was "What do you think?" After Melody put her eyes back in their sockets, she decided not to react right away. She would think about a response. She felt he had insulted her in every way possible by sending it to her. She was angry, oh yes, very angry but she stayed calm and didn't flip out at him in a quick response. After an hour passed by she responded with her answer. She wanted him to be as insulted as she felt. She was never vengeful but this angered her so much she figured he deserved an insult better than the one he'd given her. She would keep it simple and get him where it would hurt the most. It was obvious the guy was showing his most important pride and joy. She typed "Sorry, you're too small." And hit send. Then she blocked him. She found strength in standing up for herself and doing it in a dignified way. At least she believed it was dignified. She held back and didn't attack him with profanity or name calling, although she was certain he might have liked that more. She wasn't about to lower herself for the likes of that varmint!

That was the only time anyone ever disrespected her on a dating site. Most times she was respected and sometimes she might even hit up a good conversation with an intellectual man that might go on for a week or two. If he had a quick wit she enjoyed chatting even more. It was never sexual, maybe some light flirting once in a while but nothing serious. Just two lonely people talking about life. But then she would take herself off out of fear of him getting too close or if the person started pushing her too much to meet him. If there was no physical spark from their photo she didn't see the point in wasting their time meeting. She never wanted to lead anyone on into thinking there could be more. She also knew deep down she just didn't want to be hurt again.

Two and a half hours after she went back on, she opened a message that had a photo attached of a man wearing a fur hat, sunglasses, a plaid shirt, with a camouflage jacket and what looked like might be a gun strapped across his back and shoulder. There was plenty of snow on the ground. He was clearly in the wilderness and there was a ski-doo parked right behind him. It was a stunning photo taken on a beautiful winter's day. What struck her the most was his sunny smile.

There was a message attached to the photo that simply said "Hi, I am looking for someone to grow old with."

"Bullshit line!" she muttered, but she was suckered into responding, just from his smile. Melody did stay positive as much as possible but she had also learned some hard lessons from liars. She had to stay cautious and she did feel bad for the good guys that suffered because of them.

The man in the photo was definitely out in the wilderness. Grizzly Adams was her first thought but still she had not connected him right away to the reading with Phil. It was a sexy photo because his smile was so amazing! It intrigued her... "I can't see your eyes." she wrote back. Within a minute he replied. When she opened the second message, his photo literally took her breath away! "You're too good looking, you scare me!" she responded.

"Lol." he replied.

It was an instant attraction indeed! His eyes drew her in with another great smile on the second photo. Grizzly Adams on the first photo meets Rex Tillerson on the second photo, but way better looking than either. It was the hair that stood out and she remembered Phil had made a big deal about the hair. He had a beautiful head of mixed color hair, more grey than dark. It was a close up photo not showing much of his body, just the shoulders. He was wearing a salmon coloured muscle shirt and he looked in great shape. Melody was instantly smitten! She couldn't deny it. Phil's read was happening right now and it was exactly two weeks later. She was blown away at how accurate he was with the timing, never mind the rest.

"You have hot legs." Mr. Wonderful said in the next message.

"Really? That's all you can come up with after all the time I put into writing my profile?" she muttered. Her sister Delia always teased her about how much she muttered to herself, especially if she got angry.

"I don't do online sex!" she wrote back, now a little annoyed. She knew from what others had told her, there was a lot of sex going on in these dating sites. A good looking man like this would have every woman on there falling for him. She had to be smart and careful.

"Lol. It's okay, I am just saying." he replied.

"Mmhmm, sure," she murmured. "Thanks." she replied.

"Are you widowed?" she asked. His profile said he was single.

"Not as far as I know." he replied. It was the only thing Phil got wrong.

He said his name was Drake and he sent his phone number to her to text him if she wanted.

"Oh my, what do I do now?" she whispered. She noticed her leg was jittering. She put his number in her phone and sent him the first message.

They talked just about every day for the next six weeks with her constantly reminding herself not to push him away because of her mistrust issues with men. There were times she felt she shouldn't trust him but always questioned her feelings because of her past history. "Give him a chance and don't give up when you get scared." Bridgette told her. Melody filled her friend in daily. Bridgette was thrilled and not surprised Phil's prediction had come true. "He sounds like a gem to me!" She was beaming because she felt she was a part of something special that was happening for her friend.

Melody knew she had so much damage from her past it made her overly cautious but she was also now a treasure trove of wisdom too. If she could only use it wisely?! She felt connected to him from day one.

Drake was working out of town finishing up a contract. He was a heavy equipment operator. It would be two and a half months at least before he came back to Glendale where his home was. Drake had told her he wanted to see her as soon as he got back to give her a hug and she couldn't wait to finally see him in person.

Melody had asked him within the first week that they had met online, if he would send her a photo of himself giving her a thumbs up so she could feel safer talking to him. There were so many phishers online who had fake photo's up, she wanted to make sure she wasn't being set up for a scam, even though she did feel he was the real deal. His photos didn't look fake like so many tricksters had posted. With the connection she was already feeling for him, she wanted to protect herself. Within a minute she received a photo of him lying in a bed. He was completely covered to his shoulders with his blanket and giving her the thumbs up. There was a message attached which read. "I pulled my back a little when I was out shovelling. I am lying on a heating pad. S'pose you wanted to see my boobs. lol."

She burst out laughing! His response made her tear up a little too. She was not only thrilled that he truly was the person in the pictures she had seen but he was so respectful to her to make sure he was covered up before taking the photo.

She had felt an emotional connection with Drake from the very start. He sent her photos every few days of whatever he was doing, even on his day off when he went fishing. It was the new age way of connecting with someone that she was still trying to adjust to. She was the last person she knew who gave into getting a cell phone. She found them to be a menace to society most days. And now here she was texting every day with this beautiful man. Melody had never talked to anyone on a dating site before that she had instantly felt a bond with like she did with Drake.

Sometimes she felt like there was something about Drake that looked familiar to her, like she already knew him. She was certain that living in the same town they must have crossed paths at some point, maybe that's what it was? She just couldn't put her finger on it. He sent her a picture one day of him and his friend. She replied to his text and photo saying, "I wonder if I ever served either of you at a jewelry store. You both look familiar to me."

"You never know, anything is possible." he replied.

Chapter 6

WYATT'S TRUTH

Wyatt put his phone down and covered his face with both hands. He had not slept well since the day he had first contacted Melody. It bothered him that he was lying to her. Yes he was an idiot for not being up front and honest with her. He also never expected to have all these feelings for her that were now driving him crazy. How could he tell her the truth?! He knew she would stop talking to him and he couldn't let that happen.

He had recognised her right away from their introduction at the jewelry store almost ten years before. She was as beautiful now as she was the first time he laid eyes on her. Those eyes that drew him in the first time were all he could think about from morning til night. What a fool he had been. This was not the way he wanted to meet her again for sure but he was happy he did. He never forgot her. He couldn't muster up the courage to tell her yet, but he would.

It was obvious she hadn't recognized him. He had gained a few pounds and his hair had greyed. At some point he would have to tell her the truth. He just wasn't ready. He was afraid he would lose her forever this time. This was their second chance. The even scarier thing was he had divorced from his first wife but was now married again. Something he regretted and discovered after it was too late that he had done on a rebound. Somehow, someway, he would tell her the truth and fix this. She deserved better. He knew this was his chance to make things right. He would tell her the truth eventually and pray things would work out. He didn't want to go through another divorce but knew deep down it was going to happen. He was feeling like a douche bag for even being on that site and a complete failure in now having two failed marriages. He just couldn't see yet that the real failure was wasting his life by staying where he wasn't happy.

Truth be told, she wasn't happy either. Nobody really cared how many times he was married but him. He let his fears run his life sometimes and he hated that about himself. He always worried about what people think and about hurting others. Deep down he knew disappointing his family again would hurt him a lot, not because they were crazy about her because they were not, but because it would be a struggle for him to go through that again. His first divorce was painful for everyone. He was a tough guy with a gentle soul. The loneliness he felt daily was no excuse to do what he did to Melody then or now. No matter how many times he went over it in his head, people were going to be hurt. He had to be strong, fess up and see where the chips would fall.

His second wife was not what he expected. Within the first year they married it was already dead. She was as cold as ice and he felt she had tricked him into marrying her. She pretended to be loving and sexual when the truth was she hated sex and was not a nice person. She was jealous of everybody and said cruel things about people. That bothered Wyatt a lot. He wasn't perfect but never cruel. She had ruined people's lives because of her own insecurities. There were things he found out only after they were married. She had threatened him many times when they fought that she would take him for everything he was worth if he left her. He nearly lost everything in his first divorce and now he just might lose everything. It was only three years into this one and he was miserable. Yes, it was wrong for him to have put himself on a dating site just to talk to someone and no, he never expected to fall in love. He especially never expected to find Melody there.

Now what would he do with all these new feelings he was tortured with daily?! No doubt it was his fault. All he knew was that he was happy every time he heard from Melody and now they were talking on the phone. Her voice alone made him feel good inside. She was genuine, sweet and sexy as hell. He tried his best not to flirt with her too much but sometimes he couldn't help himself. He was head over heels for her. He wanted nothing more than to take her into his arms and kiss her. He would have to tell her the truth right away when he would finally get to see her in person again. He had many fears about it but had decided the right thing to do was to tell her face to face rather than over the phone. If he lost her again it would be painful and his own fault. It was hurting her he worried about the most.

Chapter 7

PUSS N BOOTS

"Hello Darling." A smile came across Melody's face when she saw the text.

"Hi sweetness." she replied.

"What are you up to?" he asked.

"I am trying to read a book but can't get my mind off someone."

"Mmmmm, I am about to go to bed."

"Me too, wish you were here! I would rub your back and snuggle with you."

"Mmmm, that would be nice." Melody felt like her body was heating up but would never let things get any hotter than this. She wanted to but was shy and not used to 'hot texting.' She loved to flirt with Drake but still held back from going too far, at least until they met in person. She was behaving herself although her womanhood was telling her she wanted to do otherwise.

He definitely had her heart and she knew once she saw him

she wouldn't be able to hold out for long before going to bed with him. She had told him several times she wanted him to take her to see the stars on a clear night for their first date. She had not been outside of town for many years camping and she missed seeing the starlit skies at night. Her other two relationships she had been in took months before she took that final step to sleep with them. They couldn't compare to this energy though, not even close. Within just a few weeks of talking to Drake she started writing in a diary about their love. She felt it would be worth keeping track of their journey, however the story might end.

"I dreamt of you last night." she text.

"Oh ya, was it a good one?"

She knew he was smiling."I think so. Do you own black cowboy boots? I dreamt you were just standing there in these fancy black cowboy boots and your underwear. Looking kind off sexy."

"Yes I do actually."

"The dream just gave me a thought about nick names that I think are cute for us. Puss n Boots." Melody added a smiley face and hit send. He made her feel childlike and happy in her heart.

She had never been called so many wonderful terms of endearment by a man as she had been by Drake. It was one of the main reasons she had fallen so in love with him over the past two months. He made her feel adored. It was amazing and magical sometimes. She still worried a shoe would drop but pushed those fears away whenever she felt doubt. She told herself it was just her own fears.

"I love it Puss! It is perfect."

"I love it too! It suits us!"

"Sweetdreams Puss."

"Sweetdreams Boots."

After taking a few minutes to write down some thoughts, Melody placed her diary on her night table and reached to turn the light out.

Only three more weeks and he would be home. Drake had told her he lived in a house only a ten minute drive from her. She couldn't wait to wrap her arms around his neck and hug him. She couldn't start thinking about him kissing her because she would be awake all night and she had to work in the morning.

Chapter 8

NAUGHTY PICTURES

It was two weeks before Drake was supposed to come home and as usual Melody was laying awake thinking about him. It was something she did every night. It seemed especially hard to get to sleep tonight because she was getting more excited as the time got closer to seeing him. He had recently sent her a couple of pictures of himself. He was partly nude in one and what she saw she liked, very much! There was nothing insulting or dirty about them. They were tastefully done. However, it didn't help her insomnia.

Melody was admittedly old fashioned in many ways. Trying to compete in this new age world of technology and people being more open with showing more of their bodies could be a struggle for people like her. Putting it all out there when it comes to nudity and photo's was not something this gal was ever going to do. Nope, never, not even if she was younger and had a perfect body! She certainly had never had any professional photos taken, partially nude or otherwise.

One week later she was lying in bed and couldn't get her brain to shut off again. Thoughts of Drake were swimming around in her head none stop again. She knew in her heart and soul she was madly in love. Some days she felt like she had not slept for more than two months since the day they first connected. Now her mind was racing! She kept thinking of a response Drake had made to her earlier that day. "I don't know if you noticed, but I am a little old fashioned?" she had written.

"I did notice." he replied. That response was now playing on her mind. As the time got closer to seeing him they had started having some very hot and heavy flirting going on. I guess you could call it sexting. Drake was definitely breaking her out of her shell. There were times her face would turn red after sending him a text that was a little more than flirty. What amazed her even more was that she enjoyed it. Melody knew she could never do it if her heart wasn't in it but it was bringing a whole new side of her out that she never knew existed. Drake had told her that he loved her many times. That had given her some kind of security because she believed him. She looked at the clock and it was three o'clock in the morning. She rolled her eyes; she would die at work later on.

Drake was staying at a friend's cabin for a few days to help repair a roof so they weren't texting as much. He did send her some nice photos of the lake. Suddenly she had an urge to surprise him. To show him, yes, she may be old fashioned but she was not a total prude.

He had asked her in their last conversation the night before to send him 5 or 6 pictures, at least that's how she understood the conversation…then he said 7 or 8? She thought she knew what he wanted and was feeling brave. Yup, she was about to do what she had never dreamed she would do in a million years. She was going to be smart about it though and do it with class. She was going to take some sexy photos for Drake. She was feeling squeamish yet a little excited that he might love them, hopefully…

Now she was not fond of the extra pounds she had put on in the past few years and was a little insecure in taking any photos of herself. She certainly had plenty of insecurities about her body but the things she got the most compliments on were her legs. Her best features were about to be the star of some photos. She got her camera ready and used her bed as the backdrop for some sexy leg photos. She covered the rest of her body with her beautiful embroidered bedding. She showed off her legs changing positions for each one she took. The lighting was really good in her bedroom so she was happy with the six she took. Nothing was revealing and they looked classy to her. There was one that made her blush that she believed showed a little too much thigh, but was still classy. She definitely wouldn't show her face in them. Even though they were for his eyes only, she knew never to take such a big risk. She was excited and a little nervous to send them! She would wait until she heard from him first. It actually made her smile to step out of her box that she had always kept so neat and tidy with a bow on top.

Melody felt okay in doing this because she loved Drake and

she felt they had a future, if not she would have never done it. They had both agreed the flirting would keep them young. She felt in her heart that this was the man she would be spending the rest of her life with. With that confidence in mind that morning, when he sent her his usual 'Happy Hump Day,' meme that he always sent on Wednesdays, she prepared to send him the first photo of her legs and she added the message, 'Happy Hump Day.'

She held her breath and hit 'send.' She then covered her head with her blanket and cringed inside questioning her actions right away. When her phone whistled a minute later she read his response. His reaction was as she hoped, he loved it! She then proceeded to send him the rest and mentioned in the message attached that he had asked for 7 or 8 a few nights before but she had only taken six. "There are only so many angles you can take of your legs." She wrote.

What he wrote back to her made her want to crawl under a rock and stay there… forever!!!!

"I read back the text from a few nights ago and it was not pictures I had asked about when I said 7 or 8." Somehow she had misread the message!

"WHAT???"

"Love the pics, thks!"

She knew he was getting a kick out of her mistake! She died a thousand deaths!! Of course he would think it was hilarious!!

"How could I have misunderstood??!! Delete them please!!!"

"Nope, they're gorgeous!!"

Her face was burning!! She just wanted to die!! "Kill me now!!"

She yelled out, burying her head in her pillow.

This horror of embarrassment lasted for all of five minutes then she quickly turned around her thoughts. Well it could be worse I guess, at least he knew she was not a complete prude and that she would go out of her comfort zone to please him. As soon as she changed her thoughts she felt relaxed about it and laughed too. Melody had learned by reading a lot of spiritual books that her thoughts have everything to do with how she felt every moment of every day. She had become accustomed to turning them around in a matter of minutes to change how she felt in different situations. The outcome could be the same but her feelings about it would not be. Drake loved the photos and if it made him happy, she was happy!

She could look back at her legs when she was eighty and remember the time with fondness and laughter on how the pictures came about and that they still looked pretty darn good for her age. They sure as heck turned each other on like crazy. That she was sure of and confident in. She longed for the day she and Drake would meet! The more anxious and excited she was about seeing him, the more the days of waiting seemed to drag out.

Chapter 9

MATTER OF TIME

Melody was cleaning a customer's ring in the back room when she heard Bridgette talking to a man. She recognized his voice right away. It was Darren the drummer in her band. She finished the ring, went back out and passed it back to the customer. The ladies face lit up from the sparkle and shine coming off the ring. She said, "Thank you very much."

"Anytime." Melody replied. The customer turned and walked away happy.

"Hi Darren, what's up?" she asked.

"Hi Mel, just wondering if you wanted to get a practice in before the dance this weekend?"

"Maybe we should. I would like to work on a new song I wrote. Why don't you call Rick and Bobby and get them to meet at my place around eight tonight if they are free?"

"Sounds good." He said as he waved goodbye.

"See you later." Melody called after him.

After work she checked her phone and there was a text from Drake. It read "I am coming home early. I will be there this weekend. I can't wait to see you baby!!" Her heart raced at the thought of finally seeing him in person! She couldn't wait to hug and kiss him. She knew the kissing would be off the charts. Intimacy was something they both admitted they missed.

"I so look forward to seeing you Boots. I am singing at a dance Saturday night. Hopefully we can see each other then or on Sunday?" He asked what time the dance was over and where it was held. "I finish at midnight at the Legion." she replied. There was no response back. "Wow, is it finally really happening?" She whispered to herself. She had tears in her eyes and her heart was bursting with joy!

It was 11 pm before the band left her home that night. They all got along well and enjoyed their practices together. They especially loved to learn new songs. Melody always felt blessed that she got to work with such professionals. It only took them going over a song once or twice to get the chords and melody down. They spent the rest of the night going over songs they enjoyed playing together. Darren did great harmony to Melody's version of Gain Control Again.

"I can't wait for Saturday night!" Melody said to them at her door. They had no idea she had other reasons for being excited for the weekend to come.

"It should be fun Mel, see you there." Bobby said as he passed by her.

Melody had another restless night but she was energized and didn't feel the pressure of getting sleep like she usually did when she had to work in the morning. She sent Drake one last text before she went to sleep that he would see when he woke up. It simply said, "WHOOHOO!"

Chapter 10

THE TRUTH IS UNVEILED

Melody was singing the Patsy Cline classic Sweet Dreams when she saw him from the corner of her eye. It was her last song of the night. The room was dimly lit but she would know him anywhere. The sight of him took her breath away. "Boots." She whispered. A smile as broad as the sun came across her face.

She had to focus to finish the song. He was standing in the back of the room sort of hidden from everyone else, leaning on a table with his arms crossed and a look so intense on his face she felt it deep in her belly. He was dressed in a blue dress shirt, black pants and black dress shoes. He looked like he had just stepped out of a GQ magazine and she knew it was for her and her alone. It warmed her heart. When he smiled at her the room lit up! He looked tanned and healthy. He was holding one pink rose, her favourite. He remembered her telling him she didn't need a dozen roses, one pink one would be enough for special occasions.

It was a shame no one else could see him but her. She finished singing the song putting all of her heart in it.

Wyatt watched and hung onto every word she sang. She sounded great and looked so damn hot! She was wearing his favourite color on a woman, a simple red dress with a slit that reached half way up her thigh. It had a scooped collar that snuggled her shoulders and the front wrapped around her breast like a gift. The black stockings she wore only made her legs even more luscious that led all the way down to her patent leather, black heels. Those soft waves of hair that ran down her back he wanted to bury himself in. "My God, what I would love to do to her!" he murmured. He just hoped he got the chance once he was free. She might just kill him and he would never get the chance. She was worth taking the risk for!

Then the reality set in again, the reality of breaking her heart! She was the sweetest woman he had ever known and the last thing he wanted to do was break her heart but he knew it was coming and he knew he had to do everything in his power to make it right and make it up to her.

Melody said a few words of thanks and goodnight to the audience and walked off the stage. Her eyes were focused directly on her man. He didn't move as he watched her walk towards him with more confidence that he ever saw in a woman in his life. She sure had come a long way from the nervous woman he remembered tripping over the containers ten years before. It killed him that he might hurt that confidence.

He stood up straight to greet her, opened his arms wide and

she rushed into them! They were both happier than kids in a candy store! You could feel the electricity in the air around them! The hug was long and tight. She heard him whisper Puss in her ear and she clung on to him tighter. They fit together perfectly. She was tall enough with her heels on to almost look him straight in the eyes. When they pulled back and looked at each other he kissed her, gentle at first and then long, hard and deep. The world rocked around them!

When they finally pulled apart, Drake passed her the rose and she brought it to her nose and smelled it. "Mmmm, thank you. You remembered." she smiled.

"You are more beautiful than I remembered Puss." He stated looking her in the eyes with an intensity that drew her in.

"Thank you Boots." she purred. She caught that he said 'remembered.' Had they met before? Drake took her hand and they walked outside.

"We need to talk." he said. Melody saw concern on his face and it worried her right away. She suddenly felt dread in the pit of her stomach and her smile quickly turned to a frown.

They walked to her car where there was a street light shining right above where they were standing. Melody looked deeper in his eyes and went to say how happy she was to finally meet him in person and a switch turned on in her memory! She recognised him suddenly and her mouth dropped open. "I met you before?"

"Yes, a long time ago."

She put her hand over her mouth as the memories flooded back to her. "But your name was Wyatt??"

"My second name is Drake, Wyatt is my first name." he said hanging his head down. He couldn't look at her. Melody suddenly felt the world spinning around her.

"Why did you use your second name?"

"I thought if I told you my first name you might remember and not talk to me. I couldn't help myself. You woke something in me I haven't felt in a very long time. Probably since the first time we met. I'm so sorry Mel!"

"You got that part right, I wouldn't have talked to you! Are you still married??" she asked. You could cut the tension with a knife! Everything seemed to be suddenly tumbling down around her! Melody was sure there had to be flames coming from the top of her head, she was so angry!

"Not to the same woman." he replied and cringed. He was finally telling her the truth and the pain he now saw in her eyes was what he feared the most. It squeezed his heart tight!

"Oh my God! Why would you do this to me, again??" she yelled at him. Now she was pacing like a mad woman in front of him.

"I'm sorry Mel, I am not happy with this woman, our marriage has been dead for a long time! Can we please sit in your car and talk there?"

Melody saw people were coming out of the Legion so she unlocked her car and got in. Wyatt/Drake/Boots, slid in the seat next to her.

Everything was spinning!! There it was, the rug was pulled out from in under her, again! Her hand gripped her dress where her heart was. "This can't be happening again!!" She muttered, now in tears. "I can't breathe!!" she gasped and put her head down to take some slow breaths to calm herself.

Everything was flooding back to her. She remembered the strong connection she had with this man ten years ago. It took her a year to stop thinking about him daily, even long after he would come into her mind and she wondered what happened to him and now, ten long years later to meet him again and she still couldn't be with him?? This was a whole other level. She had given him her heart this time!! "What kind of fucking joke is this??" she asked. She was so angry she wanted to scream at the top of her lungs!!

"I did come to find you in 2008 after my first divorce but the lady at the store said you were on vacation with your husband. When I knew you were married I didn't go back. It was a few months later when I started seeing the woman I ended up marrying. It was a huge mistake. I'm so sorry Mel!"

"How dare you do this to me again!!" she cried. When Wyatt leaned in to look her straight in the face to say something she slapped him as hard as she could across the face. She was sure his head snapped! Her hand was stinging! She was shocked by her reaction and the tears fell even harder!! They streamed down her face!!

This was so out of character for her to react like this. She suddenly felt bad for slapping him?! She went through hard times with her ex's but it never got so out of control that she ever slapped them. She was a lady of peace and common sense! Yes, she could be quick sometimes but not violent, never violent! How did this ever happen to her?! Only he could make her feel this much!

This pain was deep! Only he could bring her strongest emotions out of her! She knew he was dangerous the first time they met. She feared this might actually kill her this time! This connection was intense from the beginning. She should have blocked him from her life right away but nope, she didn't use her common sense. It seemed to have been stripped from her overnight.

"I deserved that." He said as he rubbed his cheek. "I am sorry Mel! I didn't want to hurt you but I couldn't pull myself away!"

"Who are you married to?" she asked.

"Actually the woman I am with now used to sing in town as well. Her name is Kate." he replied. Melody's eyes widened and she was about to lose her mind completely!!

"I sang in my first band with a woman named Kate! Actually, I quit the band because of her. It was my first band and I loved it. I was in it three years until I finally couldn't handle her jealousy and stunts she pulled to try to get me to quit. I couldn't handle the tension it caused in the band so I did quit and shortly after that the band fell apart. She didn't win in the end of wanting to be the queen bee! I cannot believe you would ever marry her!? She had two kids and two ex-husbands. Is that her??"

"Yes it is."

"Oh my God!! She cheated on her ex-husbands and was married at the time we were in the band and she was cheating then. She was trying to cheat with a band member who was married at the time as well. She also cheated on her husband with my sister's husband and she was working with my other sister who was so hurt and upset about the whole thing because they had been close friends. It hurt both my sisters deeply! She screwed not only me but my whole family over!!" Melody threw her hands in the air. "Why did you have to marry her, of all people?!" She was now sobbing uncontrollably! She felt like she had been kicked hard in the stomach! The hurt, anger and disbelief were more than Melody could bear! The memories of all the hurt and pain this woman caused was making this ten times worse than it already was!!

Wyatt was rubbing his head and holding back his own tears. This was torture!! Not because of the slap but because of the trauma he had caused the love of his life! "I have no idea Mel, because I respected her father I guess! Everyone at work respected him and the guys told me to date her. She pretended to be a sweet person."

"WOW, my mind is blown!! That is the lamest excuse I ever heard!! You need to get out of my car and I never want to see you again!!"

"I'm so sorry Mel." he said quietly. He now wiped tears away too. Good! She was happy he was hurting!

"Don't Mel me, get out!!" Another sob escaped her chest. She couldn't even look at him. Her heart was torn to shreds!

"No matter what Mel, I love you and I will try to fix this, I promise!!"

Wyatt tried to reach for her hand and she pulled it away and turned her face away from him. When he got out and shut the door she sped out of the parking lot glancing back at him in the rear view mirror. He was standing there with his head down and hands on his hips looking defeated. She put her window down and grabbed the rose that was sitting on the dash and tossed it out the window. She hoped he had seen her do it!

Melody pulled her car into the parking lot of the local park and got out. There was no one around this time of night and she needed to be around nature. It would give her comfort. She reached to the floor in the back of her car and pulled out her runners that she kept there for after work when her feet hurt too much to walk another step. She pulled off her heels and shoved her feet in each runner so violently she was surprised she didn't tear her stockings. When she started to walk she was a little off balance. She knew it was from her anxiety. When she reached the closest bench she flopped herself down with her hand still gripping her chest. The pain was intense and she needed to release it now or she would surely die from it! This was where she needed to be, somewhere quiet and secluded where she could let it all out!

Suddenly she felt the coolness of rain drops on her face. The harder the rain started to fall the more her heart broke and the more she released her pain! The pouring rain was beating all around her face and her body and she didn't care! It fit her mood perfectly!! Her hair was soon mangled like her heart and she didn't care!! Her perfect dress that she loved now clung to her body, soaked and ruined, she didn't care!!

She looked upward asking God "WHY? WHAT DID I EVER DO TO DESERVE THIS??" Her tears kept falling like the cold rain that surrounded her! Every time she saw Wyatt's face, the pain gripped her broken heart again and again!! She was drenched from head to toe and she didn't care!! All she cared about was the man that she loved deep in her soul was now dead to her forever!!

She fell forward with her head in her lap and she cried out!! "Booooots!! Why, why, why??!!" She sobbed uncontrollably, wishing her father was next to her, holding her and taking her pain away. She could never tell her father. He would kill Wyatt! Not because she didn't want him dead because she did, but she didn't want her father to end up in prison. The rain wasn't easing up and Melody suddenly felt chilled to the bone. She shivered and found the strength from somewhere inside to peel her body off the bench. She slowly walked back down the path to her car. Her feet were making a squishing sound from the rain that soaked her runners. She turned on the heater in her car to warm up her body that was shaking from the inside out. She drove in silence and the tears kept streaming down her face. She glanced in the mirror and hardly recognised herself. There was makeup running from her eyes down to her chin. "You stupid woman!" she whimpered.

Chapter 11

BEGGING FORGIVENESS

The phone next to Melody's bed whistled and she picked it up to read the text. She couldn't believe he had the nerve to text her after last night.

"Please talk to me Puss."

"Don't call me that! Go Away!"

"Can we be friends?"

"NO!!"

"Okay block me then, I'm fucked up!!"

"I'm not blocking you! My phone can only block calls, not text. It's an older phone. So stop texting me please!"

Melody's guard was dropping, this was not good! The thought of never hearing from him or seeing him again was now unimaginable for her. She needed to hang onto the anger!

"Okay." he replied.

Thank God it was Melody's day off so she could take the time to think and try and make some sense of what just happened. Her intuition was usually so strong. How could she have missed this? There were a couple of times she felt he may not have been telling the truth about being in a relationship with someone. When she asked him if there was anyone else he had always firmly said no. She had convinced herself she was just mistrusting him because of her past relationships! Why would she ever doubt her intuition, it was never wrong! Blinded by love! What a fool!

Last night when she got home all she wanted was to shower and go to bed. She had turned the hot water on in the shower, stood under it, closed her eyes and let the steam gather around her body. It felt good, like a blanket of comfort. She missed her sisters and her mother so much in these hard times. She needed them to talk to and to support her. She needed their hugs, and the tears fell like rain again!

"Fuck You Wyatt!!" she had cried out as she slid to the shower floor and let the water beat on her. She wrapped her arms around her body to try and comfort herself and she sobbed and sobbed for what seemed like hours. When there was nothing left she pulled herself together and washed her hair. It felt good to gently massage her head to try and relieve the headache that had set in. When she went to bed she passed out from pure exhaustion.

Melody sat on her couch now, still wrapped in her blue, terry cloth robe watching the news but she didn't hear a word of what was being discussed. She wanted to put some clothes on but didn't have the strength. It seemed like everything was so much work now, when all she wanted to do was go to bed and sleep. All her energy was drained. She had been there before after she lost her family. Depression could set in easy enough if she wasn't careful. She yearned to call her dad but she knew she would break down over the phone and she didn't want him to know. It would hurt him too.

There was a knock on her door. She ignored it and hoped whoever it was would go away but no, there it was again, even louder this time. "Cripes sake!" she whispered. She was annoyed but pried herself off the couch to see who it was.

When Melody looked out her peephole she couldn't believe her eyes.

"GO AWAY!!" she yelled.

"Mel, please let me in. I want to talk to you!!"

"I DON'T WANT TO TALK TO YOU!!"

"Please let me in for a minute!"

"HOW DID YOU FIND OUT WHERE I LIVE??" she yelled. She was furious!!

"I went to the store and Bridgette told me. I begged her for it." Wyatt sounded like he was hurting, as he should be!

"HER ASS IS FIRED!!"

"No Mel, it's not her fault. She wants you to talk to me. She said you told her about me and she wants us to work it out."

"Really? Fancy that! Work things out with a married man?? I DON'T MESS AROUND WITH MARRIED MEN!!"

"Calm down." she reminded herself. If she wasn't careful she would give herself a heart attack. She decided in that moment to let him in for a minute and that would be it. Then she would be rid of him for good! Melody unlocked the door and let him in. She didn't even care that she looked a mess. Wyatt sheepishly stepped inside, quietly closing the door behind him. He stood there looking worse than she did if that was even possible. Good, he deserved it!

Wyatt thought he would die at the sight of her. It killed him how much he had hurt her!

"Where's your WIFE??"

"She is gone to visit her son for the weekend. It was why I came home a few days early so I could see you and tell you the truth."

"Ha, lucky me!!" she spurted out with venom. She suddenly became very aware she was naked under her robe. She had to keep her distance because just the sight of him still made her heart race. Melody sat on one end of her sofa and she motioned for him to sit on the other. "Make it quick I have things to do!"

"I want us to be together Melody. I have gone over it a million times in my head and I just can't see how I can do it right now. I just need a little time." he said as he sat down.

"I already gave you too much of my time, never mind my heart, and now you want more? You must be crazy!! I don't sleep with married men, never have and never will!"

"I don't need you to; I already know the sex would be great!"

"Oh I don't doubt it would have been but it is never going to happen mister… whatever your name is this week!!"

Melody could feel she was softening up, she felt her heart was melting in his presence and she felt tears coming on. "No, cripes!" she mumbled. The last thing she wanted was to cry in front of him again. She didn't want him to know he still had a hold on her heart, but he did. He was the sweetest man she had ever met in her life and he knew how to turn on the charm to melt her heart! "Bastard!!" she said and then the tears fell. She crumbled just like that, right in front of him!! Within two seconds Wyatt was sitting right next to her and pulled her in his arms.

"I'm so sorry Puss! I'll fix this I promise!" Their lips met and she let him kiss her over and over as the tears ran down her cheeks. It got so heated she had to pull away from him several times but then she would go back for more. His hand found her leg underneath the robe. She could feel the heat from it and she wanted more! His tongue was going deeper inside her mouth and she let him and wanted him more than she ever wanted anyone else in her life! As fast as it started she pulled away and stood up abruptly!

"You have to go!" she said, pointing to the door. They were both breathing heavy.

"Will you give me a chance Mel?"

"I don't know!" she replied, trying to stay strong but feeling weak in her answer. Now she was angry at herself more than him! He nodded and said "fair enough." He walked out and closed the door quietly behind him.

She wanted him out of her heart and mind. The connection she felt with him was going to be a hard one to break, she could see that now but she had to stay strong. It wasn't going to be as cut and dry as she had thought. Usually when she was done, she was done! She had never experienced anything like this with anyone. The emotional pull was too strong for her. She hated that she didn't have more control over it! She paced back and forth remembering his kisses. Now what had she done to herself?! She just made it harder to forget him.

So this is what they wrote about in all the books. This was 'twin soul' love. It could never be this painful if it wasn't. She knew it the first time she laid eyes on him it was dangerous territory she was stepping into. Now it was too late, she was in deep and hated it because she couldn't have him unless she threw her integrity out the window completely. He may have tricked her but she would never do it. No way in hell!

Chapter 12

COMPLETE MADNESS

Three months later Melody was at work trying to stay busy to keep Wyatt off her mind. He took up her headspace constantly and she fought with it all day long, every day. Her love for him ran deep and she knew that would never change so she accepted she would live with it. It was too exhausting trying to fight it. He not only damaged any trust she had for him but for her own instincts as well. She knew even if they found a way to be together, they would both need counselling and he had agreed when they talked about it. He wanted to fix what was broken inside himself that caused him to act this way. At least he admitted that much.

Melody saw he had many good strengths or she would never have been so attracted to him. He was hard working, gentle, witty, caring, he was honest… most times, took good care of himself, loved the outdoors and loved her. He did lie about his marital status in order to win her heart. Telling a lie was always a weakness in her mind. Maybe she was looking at this all wrong? She went over it in her mind constantly and decided she could turn it around as much as she liked, it still didn't make it right and she would not be this woman that came second to anyone, ever! Especially Kate! She would be his friend but never cross the line to have sex with him. In her heart she knew deep down she had already took a step and crossed it somewhat just by letting him kiss her. She had to forgive herself for that somehow. The guilt ran deep already; she could only imagine what it would do to her self-worth if she let it go any further.

Maybe his other qualities did outweigh his bad side and would be worth the fight for Melody in the end. It was a struggle for her every day to stay sane while he was still with Kate. Trying not to think about him at all was just impossible. She could even smell his cologne sometimes. It was a constant roller coaster ride for her. When he would text her, she was like a school girl jumping to respond. If she didn't hear from him she worried. She hated it all but still loved him deeply.

Melody was walking to the mall food court to get some lunch. As she stood in line to pay for it, she saw her. "Oh my God it's her!" she gasped under her breath.

It was at a distance but she would know her anywhere. Her short and stocky build had stayed about the same and so did her hair style. Melody cringed at the sight of her, remembering how her sister had cried in her arms after finding out Kate had slept with her husband at a time they were having troubles in their marriage. It hurt her sister even more knowing Kate thought nothing of their friendship. Melody remembered when she tried to tell her family about the things Kate was doing to upset her so she would quit the band and how no one had believed her when she said this woman couldn't be trusted, until she messed with Jean's husband. It wasn't until then that the family and all their friends saw the real Kate. It had hurt Melody deeply that no one believed her. Kate had tricked them all in believing that she was a sweet person. Melody's sister Delia had to work with this woman every day and had been her best friend. It was very uncomfortable and painful for her too when she found out the truth. Nobody had ever apologized to Melody but she found it in her heart to forgive them all. Kate had fooled them just like she fooled Wyatt.

And now Kate was married to the man who was in love with her? How ironic!! It was all too crazy for words! Melody felt like maybe this was Kate's karma coming back to haunt her. She called it 'poetic justice.' She wondered sometimes if her sisters might be behind it all from somewhere above. Yet Melody couldn't figure out why she would have to suffer again in all of this?! He was a perfect match for her in the love department, yet it didn't make sense because she was being so hurt by it all. Who knows what they can control from heaven. She wished they could make Kate disappear from her memory. She didn't need these hurtful memories that had popped up again in seeing her. Wyatt may have been a good match for Melody in many ways, but the rest of the situation was a mess. The questions in her mind never ended. She was constantly looking for answers that never came. She had to try and let it rest trusting they would come eventually.

Still, Melody could not find it in her heart to be vengeful as much as she despised what Kate had done. She would never lower her standards she had for herself and sleep with Wyatt either, just to get back at Kate. It was bad enough how she already let Wyatt kiss her. She also questioned her own motives that if he had been married to any other woman, if she would have cut it off right away when she found out the truth? If maybe she wasn't getting some kind of satisfaction in having Kate's husband being in love with her? She knew the answer to this was no. She loved him completely and it would be hard to let him go no matter who he was with.

If Wyatt had told the truth from the beginning Melody would have never given her heart to him, that she was certain of. Just like the first time they met and she had felt the instant connection to him. She had told him no right away back then. The connection was off the charts back then as well but she didn't give him the chance to steal her heart. It wasn't fair for Melody to be tortured this way for nearly six months now. She also knew she was responsible for her own actions now that she knew the truth and couldn't blame it all on Wyatt any longer. No matter how much she despised Kate, she knew it wasn't fair to her either and that brought tremendous guilt to Melody daily.

This was now an opportunity for her to tip the apple cart. She could walk up to Kate and blow everything up in a second, and she wanted to… ohhh, she wanted to! She could show her just what it felt like for someone to not care about someone else's feelings. This was her chance! She thought about it for a minute. No, it wasn't her place. Wyatt had to tell her. She was not made with the same cloth as that woman, not even close. As much as she disliked her or how much she loved Wyatt, she couldn't hurt her. Even if Kate had a cold heart it didn't matter. Melody and her family had been the recipients of it. Melody knew she was certainly not a saint but she could never hurt anyone on purpose, even her worst enemy. It wasn't about courage because Melody knew she had the courage, it was about dignity and loving herself more.

It seemed routine now for Melody to be talking to Wyatt for about two weeks at a time and then the guilt would set in. The fact that he had not done anything yet to leave his wife would upset her. Melody would push him away and tell him it was over. A day or two would pass and one of them would weaken and reach out. Wyatt usually reached out within 24 hours at the beginning. Melody told Bridgette it felt like her world was falling apart whenever they stopped talking for even that amount of time. She felt panicked. It was complete madness for both of them! She wouldn't wish this dilemma on her worst enemy.

Melody didn't understand why Wyatt stuck it out in staying in touch with her knowing that she was clearly not going to sleep with him, but he did. Always saying he needed time to figure it out. Every morning, noon and night he would text her. He said sweet dreams every night before he went to bed and good morning Puss, every morning. Some days that's all Melody needed, most days she wanted more. She wanted him completely, every part of him. Sometimes she thought she might go mad with longing for him.

Melody watched Kate until she went out of sight. She hoped

somewhere down the road she could find forgiveness towards her because Melody knew that forgiveness was a huge step towards her own happiness and letting this all go. She and her father had forgiven the drunk driver that killed their family and it was extremely helpful for both of them to heal. They did it to help themselves.

Melody looked around as she walked out of the market but there was no sign of Kate now. The last thing she wanted was to have to talk to her and be fake. Even after she quit the band she was still civil to Kate whenever she saw her, as she would be now, but she didn't respect her at all. She drew in a deep breath and kept walking shaking off the heartbreaking memories.

Chapter 13

GOING OUT WITH GRACE

"I want to see you Puss."

"No!"

"Please, just to hug you. I miss you!"

"No, you have done nothing to change things. I don't want you to leave her to be with me. I want you to leave to make yourself happy. The constant complaining that she is home and how unhappy you are is growing stale. I am tired of hearing it and you are doing nothing to help your situation. I am not responsible for your unhappiness, mine alone is enough." she argued.

It was clear seeing Kate had made things harder for Melody. The phone calls between her and Wyatt were less and less the more they argued. He mostly texted her now and she rarely reached out to him first. Hearing his voice made it harder for her in missing him.

"I understand Puss, you are right." He was a man of few words, the complete opposite of Melody but they always understood each other.

"Boots, maybe this is just lust?"

"No, it's more than that."

"How do you know?"

"Because you are always on my mind and in my heart."

"Tears." she wrote back.

"Are you going out tonight?" This was a question he asked her every weekend like clockwork.

"Yes I am."

"Have fun then."

"Thanks, I will."

"Love you."

"I love you too." He was the first one to say that to her in the beginning. It seemed like years ago now. She had asked him straight out if he loved Kate when he first told her the truth that he was married and he said no, they were not even intimate. She took him at his word on this because he had promised her he would never lie to her again and so far she believed he had kept his word. Even when she asked him the hard questions and he knew she would hate the answer, he told her the truth. She respected him when he told her the truth no matter how difficult it might have been to hear the answer sometimes.

Melody knew music was who she was at her core. It was the reason her dad chose her name because music was his first love, his passion. He always told Melody she was a close second and it always made them both crack up laughing. She missed seeing him on a regular basis since he retired and moved two hours away to a retirement community. They talked and laughed on the phone often. She did not dare tell him about Wyatt. Her dad would be so hurt for her and probably disappointed she let it go on this long. One day while they were having their usual chat, her dad told her she was usually a ray of sunshine when they talked but lately he heard sadness in her voice. "What's wrong baby girl?" he asked.

"I'm fine Dad, just a little tired from work. There's nothing to worry about."

"Pick up your guitar Mel and play a couple tunes if you're having a bad day. That always turns my day around if I am down. Music brings us back to life."

"I will Dad. I agree it does."

Melody would go out with her friend Grace to hear other friends play music sometimes if she didn't have a gig to play somewhere herself. Her friends would usually get her up to sing a couple of songs with their band. It was always fun to jam with other musicians. Grace was a close friend who always had her back and she always had a fun time with her. Laughter was what Melody needed the most and she always looked forward to her nights out with her friend.

Grace picked her up at 9 pm to go to the Friday night dance. She was younger than Melody by ten years but they sure connected on a soul level. They enjoyed spending time together. This night would be no different. There was always a group of friends at the dances that they would sit with. The ladies would get up and dance the night away, sometimes a man would invite them to dance.

Melody had her limit of two glasses of wine that night and was feeling happy when Grace was driving her home. She had shared with Grace many times what was going on in her heart about Wyatt. She had been a very loyal and compassionate friend to open up and who never made her feel judged. Melody trusted her with her life. She was one of three people Melody trusted to talk to about Wyatt. Bridgette knew of course and she had confided in her other long-time friend Jenny. Jenny was a childhood friend who Melody trusted. They had all expressed their concerns for her and made clear they just wanted her to be happy.

Her friends always gave her good advice but it didn't help her a lot when Grace said "just fuck him!" It did however make Melody chuckle at how blunt Grace was. "It's not in me Grace. It's all bad enough he has my heart." Melody replied.

"Yes, but you have his as well."

"Yes I know but I want things to be done with everyone being respectful or not at all. He has to be honest with her. I don't like being in the middle of something sinister and for the life of me I can't pull away. It's crazy!"

"I get it. It just makes me sad for you."

"I'm a survivor, I'll be fine." Melody leaned over and kissed Grace on the cheek and said good night when she dropped her off at her front door. "Send me a text that you got home safely."

"Will do." Grace watched until she knew for sure Melody was inside safe and sound and then she drove home. Ten minutes later Melody's phone whistled.

"I'm home, g'nite." xx
"Goodnight luv." xx

70

Chapter 14

FACE TO FACE

Melody could feel him moving deeper and deeper inside her. She squirmed underneath him as she pulled him in closer. The kisses were wet, wild and deep. They were starving for each other! She could feel her hands running through his hair. It felt soft and silky. She could hear his moans and his voice when he asked her what she wanted. "I want you." she whispered. She heard him moan loud enough that it woke her up!

She turned over and wept into her pillow. She had this dream so many times over the past months and it was more vivid every time, like he was right there with her. Loving him and not being with him physically was torture. He had told her he had dreams of her as well…crazy dreams.

The phone whistled and she picked it up off the night stand.

"Morning Puss."

"Morning Boots."

"How was your night out?"

"It was good, I danced too much."

"Lol. That's good. I wish I could have watched you dance."

"You can, anytime you are free." she replied with sarcasm.

"Guess where I am?"

"No idea."

"I am close to your place. Can I come in for a minute?"

"NO!"

"Mel, I promise nothing will happen. I don't want to hurt you more than I already have."

"You got that right, nothing will happen!" Flashes of her dream were now running through her head. "Oh God," she whispered and covered her face with her sheet.

"Okay, give me fifteen minutes to clean myself up here."

"I will wait in your driveway."

Melody jumped out of bed, put her hair in a bun and jumped in the shower. She lathered up and washed quickly with her lavender soap. The scent helped her relax a little. She dried off and pulled on a cute casual, black pencil skirt and hauled a loose purple t-shirt over her head. She creamed her face and did a light touch of make up on her face and eyes, then quickly touched her lips with her lip gloss. She noticed her hand was shaking a little. She was so excited to see him! She let her hair down and brushed it out, took one final glance in the mirror and sent him a text. "Okay, you can come in." She took in a deep breath to calm herself.

It had been almost four months since she saw him last and she knew it would probably be another four, IF she ever saw him again. It would take everything in her not to cross the finish line today. When she opened the door it felt like all her guards came down in that very moment when she saw him standing there. She lit up and wrapped her arms around his neck. They hugged for a long time before she moved for him to come inside. They hugged again and then he kissed her over and over again. She wept and he held her tight and he let her sob in his arms for as long as she needed. "I'm sorry Puss." he said and she heard a crack in his voice. It was hard for her to always remember that he was hurting too.

"Come in and sit." she told him when she pulled herself together.

He sat on the end of her couch and she sat close to him. He wrapped his arm around her shoulder and she snuggled into him. This felt like home to her. She wiped the tears and said "What are we going to do? Is there anything I can do to help you make a decision?"

"No," he said. "You've already done enough. This is something I have to figure out. Kate and I had a big argument last night and she threatened some pretty harsh things towards me. It feels like she is looking for a reason to leave so she can take everything. She wants me to suffer. There's no doubt about that." He turned his body so he could look Melody straight in the eyes and he said. "I love you!" It was the first time he actually said it to her in that way, face to face. She was taken aback and didn't know how to respond at first.

"Well, you fucking better because I have been through hell and back!" she replied. Wyatt burst out laughing and he kept laughing grabbing her and pulling her closer to him so he could kiss her. Her heart was happy that she made him laugh so much. He always told her she was hilarious when she was sassy to him. He loved it! After he kissed her long and deep she pulled back and looked at him and said. "I love you too."

They kept holding hands and cuddling for half an hour. "Your hands are soft baby."

"Thank you Boots." When he got up to leave she wanted to cry out PLEASE DON'T GO, but she didn't.

He hugged her tight at the door and said "I'll figure something out Puss."

"Do it for you Wyatt, not for me."

"I will." he replied and left.

Later that night Melody was watching The Voice on TV and her phone whistled. She picked it up to see that Wyatt had sent her a text. "Are you watching The Voice?"

"Yes."

"Kisses." was all he wrote.

It took her a second to realize the reason he sent the texts. He was too shy to say the words to her face to face so he sent his feelings to her in a song. There was a young girl on The Voice in that very moment singing the song You Are So Beautiful To Me. As she listened to the words Melody's heart sang too and she wiped tears from her eyes.

'You are so beautiful to me. You are so beautiful to me. You're everything I hope for, you're everything I need. You are so beautiful to me.' These were the lyrics written by Billy Preston and Bruce Fisher and made famous by Joe Cocker. It was a classic that she had sung herself many times.

That small gesture Wyatt had just made was huge for her. It was probably the most romantic thing anyone had ever done for her. It warmed her heart more than he would ever know. She replied and said "Thank you, tears." with a heart emoji attached.

Chapter 15

JENNY

Another month had gone by and it was now September. It had been 9 days since Melody heard from Wyatt. She had pushed him away again and she felt this time it was over for good, although she knew deep down it would never be over in her heart because her feelings for him were stronger now than ever. She still ached for him every minute of every day as she believed he did for her. She must have picked up her phone twenty times a day, checking it in case he did text her and maybe she missed it coming in. Every day seemed like a week had gone by in not hearing from him. So many times she had said goodbye to him before but they never lasted this long. Maybe they would make it stick this time? She talked to Jenny about it when they met for coffee.

"Are you still talking to Wyatt?" Jenny asked.

"No, it's been 9 days. I think it's over." Jenny saw tears well up in her friend's eyes.

"Aw Mel," she said as she reached across the table and rubbed her arm. The sweet gesture made Melody tear up even more.

"I know its wrong Jenny, but so many times I have thought about calling and telling Kate, not because I can't stand the woman, but because she has the right to know. I can't do it. I am not sure if I would be doing it for my own selfish reasons. If they are not meant to stay together it's up to them. It doesn't matter now because he and I may never speak again anyways. I know it hurts him every time I push him away as well but it's his own fault. I just want to do things the proper way. Is that too much to ask? If he's not happy, leave! It's really that simple but I think he's scared because he went through a divorce before and I feel he went through a lot with his kids and family, never mind the financial part. I have given him more than enough time."

"Yes, that makes sense. I thought about contacting his wife and blowing things up too." Jenny said.

"Really?" Melody was surprised by this and said "I would never want you to do that for me. I really want things to go however they are meant to without doing anything that might cause more problems." It did warm Melody's heart that her friend loved her that much that she would want to do that for her.

"Yes, you're right." Jenny replied.

"The last time I talked to him he had mentioned he wanted to take me fishing before he stores his boat away for the winter. It was something I told him I always wanted to do. I said I would think about it but haven't spoken to him since."

"If you hear from him again go with him Mel, it would be a

good memory for the both of you doing something fun together, whether it works out or not." The moment Jenny said that Melody heard her phone whistle. When she checked sure enough it was him. "I miss you Puss." That was all it took. The struggle was constant and real.

Chapter 16

GONE FISHIN'

"I'm here."

"K, I'll be right out." Melody texted back.

Kate was gone to her son's again for the weekend and Wyatt told Melody he wanted to take her fishing. She reluctantly gave in but was excited to spend this time with him. She figured this one time she would try to stop worrying about everything and just have fun. She pushed the fact that it was just wrong out of her mind. It might be the only time she would get to be with him for more than half an hour. She knew in their hearts and minds they never left each other. She might go straight to hell for it but today was her day and she was determined to make the best of it.

Melody ran into his arms when Wyatt stepped outside of his truck to greet her. "Where are we going?" she asked as she hugged him tight and then passed him a basket with the lunch she had packed.

"I'm taking you up the river." He replied as he laid the basket in the back of the truck.

"Alrighty then!" she said with enthusiasm. Wyatt leaned in and planted a tender kiss on her lips. "I felt that all the way down to my toes." she said with a smile.

"Ohh, let's see if I can do it again." he replied as he leaned in again and made it last even longer this time.

"Mmmmm." she moaned.

"I better stop now or there will be trouble." Wyatt chuckled.

When they got to where his boat was launched Melody was thrilled! She didn't know if it was because she was finally going fishing or because she was spending a day with the love of her life. She imagined it was both.

Wyatt took her hand and helped her step into the boat. Melody couldn't even remember the last time she was on a boat. It had to have been twenty years. "Get comfortable. It will be about a twenty minute ride." he said.

It was a beautiful, warm fall day and Melody was going to enjoy every minute of it. As the boat sped up she hung onto her sun hat and relaxed into the warm breeze flowing over her whole body. "This feels like heaven." she said. Wyatt smiled and reached over and held her hand as he steered the boat with ease. There was barely a ripple on the water. The sunbeams were reflecting off the water and made the water twinkle. Melody lifted her sun glasses so she could take it all in. The trees along the shoreline were a multitude of fall colors already. It was spectacular!

The boat slowed down and idled. Wyatt dropped an anchor

and then he leaned in and kissed her several times. "You better quit that if we are going to catch any fish today." she laughed.

"I don't care about the fish." he chuckled.

"Well I do. I want to catch one of those walleye you're always bragging about that are supposed to be such 'good eating.'" Melody rubbed sunscreen on her face, shoulders, arms and legs. "Do you need some?" She asked.

"Sure." he replied. "You can do my arms and shoulders if you like." Melody started rubbing lotion slowly down his neck and under his tank top around his shoulders and then down his arms. She could feel every muscle flex and tense up from her touch. "How's that?" she asked. "Want me to do your legs too?"

"No thanks, I'm good. Couldn't handle that for much longer." He let out a chuckle that made her laugh. He baited the hook and passed the rod to her giving her basic instructions on how to cast it and how to bring it in if she got a bite.

"I may need your help if that happens."

"I can show you." He stood directly behind her and placed his arms around her to show her how to cast properly. Feeling him standing so close to her and gently moving her arms around to show her the motions were turning her on more than expected.

"Thank you. You feel pretty good back there." she said with a grin.

"So do you baby." he replied keeping his cool but he was getting a little heated. "I don't want a hook in the eye and neither do you so be careful and take your time Puss."

"Aye, aye Captain." she replied. They were both about to sit and relax and Melody suddenly felt a pull on her rod.

"You must be joking! Already??" she asked, unable to believe her good luck. "I might need help Boots, it feels like a big one!"

"Hang on to it baby, pull gently and then let it go for a bit, easy." Melody was holding on with all her might! Wyatt stood next to her and instructed her the whole way. When she saw it surface she squealed with excitement!

"IT'S HUGE BOOTS!!"

"Yes it is Puss, good job!!" Wyatt grabbed the net and leaned over to scoop it up for her when it got close to the edge of the boat. With all her excitement Melody gave the rod one good yank and the fish flew up in the air and smacked Wyatt right in the face. It threw him off balance and he fell backwards! Melody stood there with her mouth wide open in shock! Wyatt looked startled! He didn't know what had hit him! He looked like he was about to cry but suddenly broke out laughing and couldn't stop! "It's not funny! You could have been hurt!" Melody frowned. She had yanked on the rod so hard the fish came off the hook. Now it was flapping wildly near Melody's feet and she froze! "WHAT SHOULD I DO BOOTS, SHOULD I KILL IT??" He couldn't answer he was still bent over killing himself laughing.

"No Mel… it will calm down!" he finally said gasping for air. When the fish landed right on Melody's foot she screamed and kicked it hard over the side of the boat! Wyatt was now roaring with laughter! He couldn't pick himself back up off the seat. Melody looked at him and suddenly bent over laughing too! They were both out of control and in tears from laughing so hard!

"I give up!!" she said as she flopped on the seat next to Wyatt. Wyatt's head went back and he held his stomach trying to stop laughing!

"My cheeks hurt!" he roared. It took all of ten minutes for them both to calm down but each one of them would crack up laughing at different points of the day just from the memories of it all. "Let's eat lunch, I'm famished!" he said, finally able to take in a deep breath as he wiped the tears off his face. "You're hilarious Puss!" Every time he said that to her it put a smile on her face.

"I don't try to be."

"I know, you're a natural."

"Whew, I'm exhausted from all the excitement." Melody stated looking content that she at least hooked one. They sat and enjoyed their sandwiches and biscuits Melody had made.

"These biscuits are so good baby."

"Thank you." she replied. "They are my favourite. I have a sweet tooth so I add chocolate chips and coconut to them."

"Mmmmm mm, so good!" he said as he wolfed down a second one.

That was the deal she had made with him, if he was taking her fishing, she would make lunch. They were nibbling on some grapes when Wyatt felt a pull on his rod. He reeled in a whopper while Melody held the net this time. "That's a nice one Boots!!" she squealed.

"This one's for you sweetheart." Melody smiled from ear to ear.

Things quieted down and Wyatt looked pretty relaxed leaning back on the bench seat with the sun beaming down on his already tanned face. Melody snuggled into him. They took in the peacefulness of the moment. There were no sounds other than a loon that would call in the distance and the gentle sounds from the water lapping softly on the sides of the boat. It was almost rocking them to sleep. Wyatt leaned in for a kiss. It was tender and sweet. She wanted more. He slowly reached his hand under her shirt and she let him. Hot flashes shot through her body and their kisses became more urgent. She gently pulled his hand away and said, "Enough babe."

"Sorry."

"Don't be sorry. Believe me I want more too. Let's just relax and enjoy this moment of peace before we have to go back to reality." she said as she smiled at him. She could have stayed there forever with him.

When Wyatt dropped her off she wanted him to stay with her more than anything in the world but she couldn't risk inviting him in. Her will was strong but she didn't trust it completely when it came to Wyatt. Anytime she felt herself weaken she thought about how she might feel right after. She loved the person she was enough not to go there, even if it meant losing him completely. She already struggled enough with the guilt she felt daily. She couldn't cross the line to have sex with the man she wanted more than anything else in the world. Melody wanted him to do things the proper way so he could feel good about himself too. She knew her integrity was already damaged from letting things go as far as they had. Sleeping together was not going to solve this. She had agreed to stay friends with him but any time they even had heated texting, Melody would pull back and not talk to him for days. It was crossing the line to her and it was always a struggle and painful for both of them when she pulled away. How could something so wonderful be bad? She didn't know why he hung in there all this time without getting her in bed. She believed he really did love her. It was the reason she hung in there so long to see where it goes. Telling herself they could just be friends was foolish on her part. She knew that was impossible with the spark they shared. "I just can't invite you in, I'm sorry."

"I understand." he replied and he kissed her tenderly. It melted her to the core! "You're tough Puss." She reached out, gently placed her hand on his cheek and ran her thumb across his lips. She pulled her hand away frustrated.

"I know. Thank you for a great day."

"I'll clean the fish and drop it off for you."

"Thank you Boots."

"No, thank you for an amazing day! You sure are a beautiful woman!" They sat and just gazed at each other for a minute. They loved staring into each other's eyes. It was like they saw themselves in each other. It was the most comforting and amazing feeling. Melody was always pleasantly surprised by Wyatt's compliments. He sure knew how to make her feel good. Nobody ever made her feel beautiful before.

"Thank you." she replied.

"I love you Puss."

"I love you too Boots." He kissed her one more time, patted her on the bottom and chuckled as she climbed out of his truck.

Three hours later he knocked on her door and handed her a container with a perfectly filleted walleye. "You are awesome! Thank you!"

"You're welcome, enjoy." She gave him a heartfelt hug. She wanted to make him a meal too but thought better of it. She knew it might turn into some kind of hanky panky in the kitchen. He was looking pretty fresh and sexy though in his blue jeans and black t-shirt. As he was walking away she suddenly changed her mind. It just didn't seem fair to her to have him catch the fish and clean it and not at least invite him to dinner. She called after him… "I will make you a meal under one condition. You stay three feet away from me the whole time you are here?"

He swung around quickly and marched back towards her. "I promise." he said with a grin. She gave him a look as if to say she doubted his promise. Deep down it was her she worried about the most. She knew he would never go any further than she wanted to.

Melody carried the fish to the kitchen and she started prepping the meal. Wyatt stood on the other side of the island and said. "I'm not going to get in your way but you let me know if I can help."

"I may ask you to chop a few veggies for a salad if you don't mind. I can manage the rest."

"Sure thing. Well this is special, us making a meal together."

"It would be even more special if we could make out while cooking but the only thing cooking in here today is your catch of the day. You just remember that!" she replied with a smile and a stern look in her eyes. Melody poured a glass of wine for herself and one for Wyatt. As she passed him the glass their fingers brushed. "Cheers," she said.

"Cheers baby."

"Do you prefer rice, mashed potatoes or fries with your fish?"

"Either way is fine with me Puss." he replied. She sliced the potatoes into fries, tossed them in olive oil, garlic powder, salt and pepper and slid the pan in the oven. She then put oil in the frying pan and let it heat up. She lightly coated the fish with flour to give it a crust and kept it simple with a sprinkle of salt and pepper for flavour. The pan was hot and the grease splattered when the fish hit the pan.

"Perfect." she said as she took another sip of wine. She opened her fridge door and took out lettuce, tomatoes, a cucumber and celery. She passed them and a chopping board to Wyatt. When she passed him a knife to chop with, he touched her hand and she felt she had to hold herself up by leaning on the counter. Wyatt could feel the electricity too, even with an island in between them.

"You okay Puss?"

"Yes… I'm fine." she stammered. He sat on one of the stools and started chopping, making jokes about how great she looked in the kitchen. He made her laugh constantly. She loved that about him. She watched him chop the tomato perfectly.

"This is not your first time doing this?"

"I was a cook's helper in a restaurant when I was a young man, was one of my first jobs. I chopped plenty of veggies in my time."

"Wonderful! Keep chopping and please turn over the fish in a few minutes while I quickly jump in the shower. I need to wash off the suntan lotion from today." Melody could tell from the aroma coming off him and floating around the kitchen that he had showered before he came over. It was getting to her in places she had guarded and was off limits. "I can do this." she whispered, rolling her eyes.

"No worries go ahead Puss. Need me to wash your back?" he chuckled.

"I think I can manage." she smirked and headed for the shower. Fifteen minutes later she returned with her hair down and wearing black leggings and a loose fitting, red top that had a little lace going down the front and with peek-a-boo arms. She didn't think it was too revealing.

He could smell the scent of her lavender soap which was more than enough to drive him crazy. He was almost panting at the sight of her.

Melody couldn't believe he had already set the table and had everything ready for them to sit down and eat. He had even lit the candles on the table. He refilled her glass of wine and pulled out her chair. "I know I promised to stay three feet away but I have to be gentleman." he said.

"Thank you babe. Everything looks wonderful." she said as he sat directly across from her. "Mmmmm, this walleye is delicious Wyatt, cooked perfectly. Now I know why you love it." she stated after she tasted her first bite.

"It's even better because you made it Mel." he said and smiled at her. She could tell he was being genuine.

"We made it. Love the salad too."

Melody took this time they had together to ask him many

things about his childhood and he asked her things he was curious about her. They kept the conversation light. They didn't want to talk about anything too serious that might ruin the mood. Neither took their eyes off each other the whole time. Wyatt knew she moved him emotionally and opened him up to tell her things about his childhood that he never shared with another soul. She was happy he trusted her completely. She was compassionate, non-judgemental and kind and in this short time they spent together they got to know each other on a whole other level.

"I have to ask you a question about something that happened that first time we met that I have always been curious about. You don't have to answer." she said.

"Go for it."

"When you came to the store to see me for the third time ten years ago and you left without saying a word, what were you going to say to me?"

"Hmmm, well, thinking back I just remember wanting to apologize for upsetting you when I had been there before and to tell you my wife and I were separating. When I saw the look in your eyes I couldn't do it. I just felt at that point I didn't have a chance. My nerves got the better of me. It turned out it took another five years to finalize the divorce. I sort of gave up for a while after I saw you that last time. I sure wish I would have told you no matter how it turned out."

"It's okay and I understand. I remember I was more shocked that you came back than anything. I wasn't angry at you anymore, although I may have come across that way. If most of us could turn back the clock I believe the majority of people in the world would be living completely different lives. I also believe what we go through is part of our path to grow and is meant to happen."

"I believe you may be right Puss."

After finishing off her second glass of wine Melody didn't realize how much it had affected her until she stood up to clear the table. Wyatt jumped up to grab her arm when she swayed. "Oh no, I'm fine." she giggled knowing it was the wine. "This is why I never drink more than two glasses." His smile did her in. All her fences came down and she stepped towards him and wrapped her arms around his neck. Wyatt wrapped his arms around her waist and held her tight. Don Gibson was singing Sensuous Woman on the radio and Wyatt started slow dancing with her.

"Not sure this is a good idea Boots." she whispered, as she leaned into him. He was a great dancer. She looked at him, kissed him tenderly at first and within seconds the kisses became urgent. Melody felt like she would melt like a flower under a heat lamp in his arms. He brought her in tighter and she knew right away he was feeling it too. She opened her mouth wider to welcome his tongue. It was intense!! She suddenly pulled away and she took his hand. "Come with me." she said. She led him to the couch. He sat and she straddled him. Wyatt couldn't believe what was happening. God he wanted her more than he ever wanted anyone but after only minutes of caressing her body and feeling he could take her right there, it was he that stopped it. He knew with her drinking she was going further than she would ever have allowed if she wasn't and she would regret it. He didn't want to hurt her even more.

"I have to go baby." he moaned.

"No, please stay." she begged. "I just want to kiss you and snuggle, nothing more." she pouted.

"I can't handle it Mel and you're not yourself."

"Yes, you are right." With her body still on fire she found the strength to pull herself off him and she sat next to him. He wrapped his arm around her shoulder to snuggle. "Please stay awhile to hold me?" she asked and he did. Melody fell asleep in his arms. When she woke up in the morning she looked around and he was gone. He had covered her with a blanket. She went to the kitchen to find he had cleared away the dishes. There was a note left on the island that read. "Good morning darling. I wish I could have done more for you to make you happy. Thank you for the lovely meal and wonderful memories. I love you, Boots." xx

She sent him a text. "Thank you for cleaning up and for the best day of my life! Love you too. Puss." xx

She lay her phone down. She knew this happy feeling wouldn't last long before the sadness would set in again. She would at least keep the good memories of an amazing day with her. They would also torture her even more. She knew she could be her own worst enemy sometimes.

Chapter 17

SONG FROM THE HEART

It was the typical winter storm outside. The wind had picked up and Melody could hear the tree limbs brushing against the side of the house. She was sitting on her couch with the fireplace crackling to warm her. She pulled her wool shawl tighter around her shoulders to help shut out the chill that ran deep for more reasons than one.

She had a big argument with Wyatt in the morning and she was still hurting from it. The thought of never hearing from him again was more than she could comprehend. Her head hurt, her stomach hurt and her heart hurt more than she ever imagined. She wasn't ready for the end and she could see no light for a real beginning with him. He wasn't willing to take the risk. It saddened her to the core. Yes, he had taken a beating with his first divorce but she saw no reason why they couldn't be together. He kept putting up obstacles with his own fears. "I don't want to talk about this anymore, and I don't want to hear from you anymore!" she clearly stated before she hung up on him.

It was also clear she was feeling more than down today. Her mood matched the weather outside and made it easy to write a heart breaking song. Most songs came to her quickly when she took the time to sit and write one. It was always healing for her to release how she felt. This one was no different. It took her all of ten minutes to write the first draft. She took another ten minutes to change a few words and get the melody down. She was now ready to record it on her phone. Her dad always told her, if it doesn't come from the heart people won't connect. This one had definitely come from her heart.

"How much more depressing can you get then this?" she mumbled. When she sang it every word pulled on her heartstrings. She loved the melody and sang it with the same feelings that were causing her so much grief in her heart. She titled it, Loving You.

> You lie there dreaming while you sleep
> She watches you, while I weep
> I can't go on loving you
> Cause my heart feels so blue
> What's the reason you're with her
> Tell me again, it's me you prefer...
> Loving you, loving you
>
> You're on my mind day after day
> She gets to hold you 'cause you stay

Telling me you love me so
My love for you only grows
Your sweet kiss, it should be mine
I'll keep pretending I am fine...
Loving you, loving you

Bridge:
Where do I go, who'll hold me tight
When I call your name every night
Darling take my hand, take the lead
When my heart bleeds, when my heart bleeds...

Another dawn has turned to dusk
I tell myself, I simply must
Forget about you, tell you no
Too many seasons will come and go
But deep inside my soul can see
This love is for eternity, so I'll go on...
Loving you, loving you
So I'll go on...
Loving you, loving you

Melody turned off the recorder on her phone, put her guitar back on the stand and went to bed heartbroken and ready to finally let him go. She already knew the routine. She would cry him out of her system. Hopefully it would not take forever.

Chapter 18

A DAD'S HEALING LOVE

Her phone whistled with a text from Wyatt. Melody turned the sound off. She had deleted two text from him already without responding. He said he wanted to talk to her but there was nothing left to say in her mind. She had called Bridgette and asked her if she would take care of the store and call in other staff for the week. "Are you okay Mel?" Bridgette asked. "You sound terrible."

"I just need some time to get past this, whatever it is." Melody didn't have the strength to explain and Bridgette didn't push her.

"Don't worry about a thing Mel and I am here for you in whatever you need. Just call me, okay?"

"I will, thank you luv." Melody whispered, trying her best not to cry. She had done way too much of it lately. She hung up before Bridgette could say another word that would make her break down completely. She buried her head in her pillow and went back to sleep.

The dreams were never ending. There was many of her loving him the way she wished she could. There were dreams of despair too. She woke up from those feeling gutted!

For three days she barely ate and only got up to use the bathroom, shower and then go right back to bed. Her bedroom was usually such a bright and cheery place with soft colors to brighten it even more. Now it was in complete darkness to suit her mood. She kept the blinds down and had pulled the drapes closed to shut out any possible light from getting in. This was her time of letting go. She had to let herself feel all the pain before she could move on and it hurt big time!

The week before Christmas she had told Wyatt she was giving it one year, that was it! January 25th was going to be the end one way or another and it was no doubt tearing them both further apart. He had pulled away as well. This might go on for many years if she didn't take the reins and get some kind of control back in her life. Many days she felt she was lost in the situation with Wyatt. She had told him on the phone "Something has to give. I can't go on like this." With every little change she felt her heart break even more. He had avoided answering her questions and started texting her less and less. No more sweet dreams and fewer good morning texts. She hated putting pressure on him. She would rather just walk away. It wasn't easy for either of them. Yet he still sent her text to make sure she was okay.

The week after Christmas he had wrote a text to her when she questioned his mood change that simply read, "It's not fair for me to keep you hanging on if I am staying where I am. Your integrity is intact." There it was, he had made a decision. The easy one! Now she had to be strong and cut off all ties with him.

Melody had told him from the beginning when he first admitted he was married that her integrity meant everything to her. She liked the person she saw in the mirror every day. Her self-worth was something she worked on her entire life and she would never want to tarnish it to have a sexual affair with him or any married man. It was bad enough that he had her heart. In a normal situation that would have been a great thing. He was the one married, not her. The choice was his to make and he didn't choose her. She had to walk away for good! She had tried to imagine many times what it would have been like for them both if they had met and he wasn't married. It was something she only dreamed of.

She was now blaming herself, typical woman thing that made her angry. She had pulled away from him so many times over the past year because she knew it was wrong to love a married man this way and now it finally felt like it had ended for good. She had to keep reminding herself that she would never have let herself fall so hard for this man if he would have simply told her the truth from the beginning, like he had the first time she met him eleven years before. She had to let him take the brunt of the blame if there was any to be given. And yes, she could have walked away completely when she found out the truth but it was too late, she had already fallen deeply in love with him. God knows she tried many times to stop it. He had begged her to stay friends with him and she did because of her own feelings. She also had to stop making excuses for them both. The whole thing was just wrong!

Many times when she asked a question and he didn't give her straight answers, it caused her to overthink everything. She always needed answers to put her worries to rest. Melody was someone that liked to have control of her life and her emotions but as she learned many times already, nobody has that kind of control. Trying to constantly avoid getting hurt was impossible. She was a risk taker; Wyatt was not when it came to their love. That hurt a lot! In her soul she believed they should be together but had to accept there was a reason they were not. She had to stop going over it in her brain and driving herself crazy. She had to give all control back to God. She trusted He always had her back. She would move on and put all her faith in Him. Whatever plan He had made for her she would follow.

Melody was drifting off again when she heard a knock on the door. It seemed distant, like it might have been a neighbour's door. Again she heard it, louder this time. She didn't care, she wasn't answering it. Whoever it was would go away. A few minutes later there was a tap on her bedroom window and she heard her father's voice call out. "Mel, are you there?"

She shot up in the bed! She couldn't believe her dad was there. Melody threw the covers off, jumped out of bed and rushed to the window. When she pulled open the drapes and the blinds sure enough, her dad was standing there and waving with a big smile on his face. It melted her heart. "I'm coming Dad, go to the front door!" she yelled. She pointed in the direction to make sure he understood. He acknowledged her with a wave and turned to walk in that direction.

Melody hurried to open the front door and her father stepped inside and quickly closed the door behind him. "It's freezing out there." he said as he took off his gloves. When he looked at his baby girl all he saw was grief through her painted on smile. He grabbed her and hugged her tight and she collapsed in his arms. "Dad." was all she could get out before she sobbed uncontrollably.

"I'm here honey, I'm here." he whispered, as he held her in his arms. He walked her over to the couch, sat and held her and he let her cry on his shoulder. "It will be okay sweetheart. I know it doesn't feel that way now but it will be, I promise." he said as he rubbed her arm. She couldn't speak. She just let everything she had left in her release in that moment. The grief had been deep. It was not the first time her father had seen her this way. She was the same when she lost her mother and sisters. She was bedridden for days. Her father hated whenever she cried, it broke his heart too. He wiped away his own tears.

"I'm going to make you your favourite, tomato soup and a grilled cheese sandwich. How does that sound?" he asked when he felt she settled down. He could see she had lost a few pounds and it bothered him.

"Sounds great! Thank you Dad." She hugged him tight before he got up and took off his coat. "How did you know?" she asked.

"I couldn't get an answer on your phone so I called the store and Bridgette told me a little bit about what was going on, so I had to come. I was worried."

"I'm sorry to worry you but I am happy you are here. I feel a little better already." she said wiping the remainder of the tears away and blowing her nose into her soggy tissue. Her dad smiled at her and got to work feeding his girl.

After Melody got dressed into her daywear, she sat with her father and ate. "Mmmm, this is so good." she said as she slurped up every bit of the soup before she dug into her sandwich. It was weird how she had not even felt hungry over the past few days until now when the food sat in front of her.

They played checkers in front of the fire. Something they did often since she was a child. She rarely beat him but there was always plenty of chatter and laughter. She needed this now more than ever. The light was coming back to her, slowly but surely. How blessed she felt to have a father that made her feel so loved. She told her father the truth about what happened with Wyatt and she felt relief by finally purging it all to him. He understood but was hurt for her. He was upset that Wyatt had lied to her at the beginning. He also understood that people meet and fall in love. It was normal, something we can't control but being honest and having courage was crucial in these situations for everyone involved. He told her he hoped she would at least feel good in the end that she didn't cross the big line. "Most people would, with no thought about the repercussions later. I am proud of you for that. I know it had to be a real struggle for you because you clearly love him. There are people who have open marriages these days, I wouldn't want to live that way but at least it's honest and no one gets hurt. You would have to be a pretty cold person to be okay with that and that's not you. You wear your heart on your sleeve.

Don't ever feel bad for having a good and soft heart Mel. We are all different." he said in a tone almost like he had experienced it before, but she wouldn't ask. She wanted to see her father as perfect but she also knew nobody was perfect. Like Wyatt, nothing her father could do would ever change her love for him. "I could wring his neck though." Melody heard him mutter.

"I don't blame you Dad. Many times I wanted to do the same." she chuckled.

He was sure proud of her that she had stuck to her guns, as hard as it was. By day three of his visit he was ready to leave and give Melody her space back. He knew she would be okay now. She was a strong lady. "Any man that deserves my daughter should have to work for it and do the right thing!" he stated firmly.

"I agree!" Melody said as sternly as her father had. They both hugged each other tight as they said goodbye. "Thank you for coming, please drive safe. I'll be okay now. I have to get back to work." she told him. Melody loved her father more than anything. He was all she had left and would surely die if anything were to happen to him.

"I will give you a call when I get home." he said. She watched as he walked to his car and turned to wave to her. She felt a tug on her heart knowing she would miss him now more than ever.

Chapter 19

THE WATCH REP

Melody had checked her phone while her dad was there and she saw she had many text and phone messages from Wyatt. She had not read a text from him or listened to any of his voicemails. It could wait until she was ready. She felt she had let him go now in her mind as much as she possibly could, although she knew he would never leave her heart. Anytime he came in her mind she practiced shutting it down right away. This technique she had learned in a self-help book and it worked if a person was strong willed enough to stick to the program.

She stayed busy at work for the next two weeks and gave Bridgette some deserved time off. One day a man walked into her store that she had never met before. He introduced himself as Martin. He shook her hand and said he was the new Bulova watch representative. He was dressed in a dark suit and a brown, open neck shirt. He was tall and handsome and he knew it.

He showed Melody a line of new watches for her store. She bought them all and thanked him. "Are you free for dinner later?" he asked as he shook her hand again before he left. She was taken aback by his boldness and said, "No, but thank you." He flipped over one of his business cards and jotted his private number on the back.

"If you change your mind send me a text or call anytime. I think you are stunning!"

"Thank you." Melody muttered taking his card. It had been awhile since she was asked out and she appreciated the compliment. Melody never thought of herself as beautiful much less stunning. She always thought of these men that pass out compliments right away as players. He didn't hide that he was and for some weird reason she admired that about him. That was honest. The fact that he asked her out was a good sign that she was no longer giving off the vibe that she was already taken. Her heart had been taken, but not her. She was certainly free to love again but had already decided she was done in that department. She was just fine on her own.

That night when she was sitting at home reading a book, she was having trouble focusing and gave into picking up her phone and reading the text from Wyatt. She wasn't ready before now.

"I am an asshole Puss." was the first text she read.

"Yup, you are." she muttered. There was one that said he was sorry for hurting her. There were several more that simply asked if she was okay. Then she listened to the voice mails, each one saying the same things that he was sorry, that he loved her. When she finished listening to the last one she decided to delete them all and not respond to any right away. She needed to give it some thought as to what she should say to him. She knew there was only three days left now until the 25th when the one year would be up. She would respond to be polite so he didn't worry and then end things for good. In her mind she had already let him go. It was her heart that was still fighting to hang on. Her intention was never to make him feel pressured but that she had simply had enough. She was a number one in her mind, never a number two. And that would never change.

Chapter 20

THE FINAL CALL

Melody sat on her couch holding her phone in her hand for what seemed like an hour. She just stared out the window. It was the most beautiful sunny day outside. She could see clear across to the hills in the distance. The snow was glistening that had fallen the night before. Everything looked bright, fresh and new. Her heart was anything but bright and fresh. It was in a ball, tight and painful. She had to make this last step even though she was afraid of the answers.

"Can I call you?" she finally typed and hit send. Two minutes later her phone whistled.

"I am driving. Give me a few minutes until I get on the divided highway."

"Okay." Within five minutes her phone rang and she picked it up. "Hi"

"Hello, how are you?"

"I'm okay" she replied. "Where are you?"

"I'm just driving back from my friend's cabin. Are you okay?"

"Yes, I'm alright now. My dad came to visit for a few days."

"Nice!"

"Did you catch any varmints today Jed?" she asked with a chuckle. She wanted to lighten the mood and Jed and Granny was something she had started with him months before when he was out hunting with his friends. He brought her silly side out for sure and he always went along with it.

"Not today Granny." he laughed.

"Boots, I have to be serious for a minute." There was a pause.

"Okay."

"I know we tried ending things before and it never worked, but this past month we have drifted further apart. Despite your texts apologizing, nothing has changed has it?"

"No. Sorry about all the texts but I was really worried about you Mel."

"It's okay. You already said you are staying where you are so we do need to say goodbye."

"Yes Puss, I see no way out for me. I'm sorry." Melody felt her chest tighten and felt the tears coming. There was nothing left to say.

"We can't have any more contact. Don't worry about me, I will be okay. I already let things go as much as I could. Now I just have to process it all. I just don't know why this had to happen to us twice now. We've had two chances at this." she said and a quiet sob escaped her heart. "Goodbye." She didn't want him to hear her cry. She just wanted to hang up. There was just a mumble of goodbye from him as he stumbled over his words and the phone went dead. She let herself cry just for a minute to release the pain and then she stopped.

How easy it would be to break him and Kate up. Even now she still thought of it daily, knowing deep down she never would. Kate would do it to someone in a second. Melody would never want a man to be with her because she had manipulated it in any way. If they would ever be together as a couple, it would have to be because he came to her willingly and honestly. It would take great courage which she knew he had, but he didn't know it. She believed in him a lot but it didn't seem to help him.

Melody knew she obviously had a weakness she needed to strengthen inside of her to have let this go on for so long. She had, however, shown how strong she really was by keeping the better part of her integrity intact. He didn't push her and she did feel Wyatt respected her in many ways. She did regret how far it went at her home when he was there but he had stopped it. She would have to forgive herself for letting things go on this long. She hoped she was finally over the worst of it. What was broken inside of him and his wife was not her concern to fix.

When Melody went to bed that night she said her prayers like she did every night, always asking God for knowledge, guidance and truth. She felt something had already changed inside her that made her feel lighter. She had to make sure she took care of number one. She was calmer than expected after the call. There were no more tears that night.

Chapter 21

THE FINAL EMAIL

The next morning on January 25th, one year exactly from when Wyatt first contacted her, Melody woke up and sent him a text. "Morning Boots, I still have questions I need answered. I pray the answers will come. No need to respond, I will figure it out and let you know when I do. It may help you too. Take care."

"Morning puss, I am going fishing."

It struck her funny that he seemed to act like nothing had changed. She could tell by his response that he didn't take her serious. He was still hoping she would hang on to him, even though he already told her he was staying where he was. That was sad to her. Why would she? She didn't want to give him a glimmer of hope just because of the text. She had to just let the answers she needed to come to her. She had prayed for it. She had to figure this out today because she was determined to move on for good. It was amazing that what she had said to him before Christmas about only giving him one year of her life and how it ended up being to the day. To know she would never hear from him or see him again was too much for her to think about, so she didn't. She pushed the thoughts away like she had practiced. She had told Wyatt before that he had turned her world upside down, and he did in so many ways, not all good. He was the love of her life but all of her hopes were gone now. Melody fell back to sleep and had a dream. When she woke up she knew she would soon have the answer she had prayed for. Something about the dream had awakened something inside her. She just wasn't sure what it was yet.

Shortly after getting out of bed it became clear to Melody what she needed to do to end this in a healthy way for both of them. Writing would give her all the clarity she hoped for. She never planned or knew what she would write until she sat in front of her computer and started typing. It just flowed with no thought or effort when she was inspired. She knew this kind of writing came from somewhere else. It was spiritual.

Melody stared at her computer for a moment. She clicked on Wyatt's name to forward the email to him. Without any thought she started typing and it flowed. What came out of her she didn't expect, but she got her answers…

Hi my darling,

I am writing this email because I have too much to say to write it in a text and I know if I called you I would get emotional and I don't want to put you through that. This is a good email so don't cringe. lol.

I went back to sleep this morning after I sent you that text.

Sometimes when I put something out there, the answer will come to me. Why we connected again one year ago today was my biggest question. I felt there was a reason more than falling in love.

I had a dream when I fell back to sleep. My two sisters were in it. I can't remember what it was all about but the moment I woke up I started thinking about what blockages I was carrying that are stopping the things I want the most. It is something I have been learning along the way about spirituality. I don't always realize when I am bringing something negative to myself, although I will never see you as a negative but the fact that I can't be with you the way I want, is a negative in my mind.

I need to forgive Kate, not only on my behalf but on behalf of my family as well. That is the negative blockage in my heart. I never hated her but definitely had negative feelings for her, for sure even more so now because she has you. It was just another dagger in my heart to find that out so many months ago. Sooo, I had a chat with God, an honest tearful talk.

I forgive her for what she did to me and to my family. I forgive you for lying to me and most importantly I forgive myself for hanging on to those feelings of resentment towards her for all this time and for staying in this even after you told me you were married. It is the hardest thing to do, to forgive ourselves but it's so necessary to live a healthy, happy life. I didn't realize until you that this experience was possibly for me to come to this place of forgiveness for this one woman on earth that I still had hidden distain towards. I've learned a great lesson here…

I feel my sisters are proud of me today and I believe they already knew the answer where they are. Somehow they directed me in my dream. Everything makes sense to me now. They would want me to forgive her on behalf of them as well. Our journey here is to grow, learn and evolve into better people.

I want you to forgive yourself for lying and hurting me. You are a good person in so many ways. We all have flaws and weaknesses.

I will love you forever and ever, that I can't change, so why fight it. I will always be friendly towards Kate if I ever see her. I always did after our band break up but now it will be honest. I suddenly feel like sunshine!

Puss xx

PS. Send me one final text to let me know when you read this please.

Two hours passed by and Melody finally heard her phone whistle. "My stomach is in knots." she muttered, not knowing how he would respond to her email. He might think she was crazy with the spiritual stuff but she had wrote it from her heart. That couldn't be a bad thing. She picked her phone up and opened it. Sure enough there was a text from Wyatt.

"Hi, I read your email….besides a wonderful person and a great writer you are amazing puss! I love you!" x

She put the phone down and wiped away the tears that escaped.

Chapter 22

FIVE YEARS LATER

Five years had passed since Melody's final email to Wyatt. There had been no contact since then. Where had the time gone? She had made some big changes in that time. She sold her business over a year ago and made enough money to buy her dream cottage by a lake just a half hour drive from Glendale.

Some days were still a struggle for her but at least now she was not only content but happy where she was. She felt she had made the right choice in cutting off all contact with Wyatt. It seemed so long ago now.

Many times for the first year she picked up her phone and looked at his picture still next to his number, yearning to call him but would talk herself out of sending him even one text. She would push the thought away. She knew from their past, that's all it would take from either of them to start communicating again. Deep down she knew there was no point. She won the battles she fought inside herself and eventually got a new phone and new number putting her old phone to rest.

Bridgette had tried to get her to date other men but she lost all interest after Wyatt. He had been the love of her life and she was done. She also believed in her heart that as long as they were both still alive they would come together again somehow, someway.

Bridgette had suggested she should maybe call Martin the sales rep. He had been in their store many times and anyone could see he was smitten with Melody. She thought he was a good match for her friend but Melody was not feeling a spark with him at all. "He's not for me Bridge."

"How do you know if you don't even try?"

"I don't need to try, I just know."

"Well, if I wasn't already taken I would give him a run for his money. I think he's hot!" Melody rolled her eyes at her friend.

"Oh cripes, will it never end?" she chuckled.

"Not until you call him. I know he really likes you. He drools every time he comes in the store Mel."

"He's too arrogant for me. Let's leave it at that." Bridgette knew she should stop pushing Melody but it broke her heart every time she looked at her.

"Even when you're smiling I can see sadness in your eyes."

"I'm great! Don't worry about me Bridge. My work keeps me happy." she had said. She hugged Bridgette for caring about her so much.

Melody was happy with her decision to stay single. No more heartbreak for her. She had had enough for a lifetime. She sure missed working with Bridgette though. They had many good times together and although they saw each other a lot less often, she was still a good friend to her.

Melody had now set herself up in a beautiful and peaceful place. Her cottage was one thousand square feet. She had more room than she ever needed. She had it updated with all the modern conveniences before she moved in, keeping the original features as much as she could. The outside of the cottage looked welcoming and cozy with the sky blue paint she had chosen and the white shutters. The front door she had painted a soft yellow. The stained glass along the top and sides of the door was colourful. It made the entrance welcoming and stand out even more. The contractors did a wonderful job in saving it. There were many beautiful wood features throughout the inside. It was finished with Melody's touches everywhere you looked. It was warm and cozy. There were soft colors of creams, blues and greens throughout. The living area looked out over the lake and had a big stone fireplace that she enjoyed and appreciated during the cold weather months. The kitchen cabinets were painted a cream color with a sage green island and brushed brass finishes. She had top of the line antique white appliances that looked old school but were modern and convenient. She loved to cook for her friends on occasion.

The most important thing was the view. It was stunning! There was a big slider door that had a clear view of the lake. On a sunny day with blue skies as the backdrop the view captured her heart and inspired her. Even on a cloudy day she loved to sit and watch the sky. Melody had the deck extended and spent every beautiful day on it, either writing songs or doing her artwork outside. She had even taken it upon herself to start writing a book. Something she had dreamed of but never thought she could do. Wyatt had always told her she should. He thought she had a way with words. That gave her the incentive to at least try it. She hadn't touched it for months though. It seemed her inspiration had gone away. Now she didn't think she would ever finish it.

There were perennial flowers that blossomed and smelled amazing in the spring and summer time. They were planted all along the deck and in rows along the path to both entrances. The many rose bushes, lavender and daisies were her favourite when they were in bloom. The fragrant smells were intoxicating and relaxing.

There was a local market every weekend for all the artists in the community and she attended them all. She loved the sense of community and the people there. She had made many friends. There were two women she had met that she considered trusted friends now that she could confide in, which she did every time they came to visit her for coffee or dinner. Sometimes they came to see her latest art work before anyone else could. They had bought several of her paintings already. She felt uncomfortable taking their money but they always insisted. They were her closest neighbours as well. Fiona was ten years older than Melody and Eileen was seven years older. They were always fun to be with and helped her in so many ways with their good advice and wisdom. Fiona was divorced and Eileen was a widow. Sometimes they would all go out to the little community pub and the three of them would walk home together along the beach laughing and giggling the whole way like young school girls. The topics were usually little stories about life in general and there were many about men from their past. Although she had told her new friends a little about Wyatt, she steered away from talking about him as much as possible. There was no point in dredging it all up again. His memory was tucked away in her heart.

Sometimes when they were together they would share stories and tears over lost loved ones. Melody felt like she had gained two more sisters and believed her meeting them was no accident. They certainly had a soul bond. She still stayed in touch with her other best friends Bridgette, Grace and Jenny on a weekly basis. She had no shortage of good friends and she appreciated every one of them.

Melody used a lot of pastels in her artwork. She would sell one or two pieces of art at every event. What more could she ask for?! She felt blessed and grateful in so many ways. Her favourite piece of art hung over her bed. It was of a woman and man embracing in a dance. Yes, it looked a lot like her in Wyatt's arms, but she would never tell. The soft colors matched her neutral bedding that had accent pillows of blue and green with some soft yellows to add a little contrast to the bedding. She had her antique bedroom set stripped and painted an antique white, trimmed with walnut color tops. She had shelving built next to her fireplace that held her multitude of precious reading material. She spent many nights sitting in front of the fire curled up with a good book. This was the good life she had always dreamed of. She loved every nook and corner of her home that felt so warm. There was only one thing missing that always put an ache in her heart but she controlled that ache now, it didn't control her.

Chapter 23

FREE AT LAST

Wyatt was chopping fire wood and his friend Roger was stacking it in perfect rows along the fence. Roger was going on about the great time he and his wife had at a friend's wedding over the weekend. "You think you'll ever marry again Wyatt?"

"Nope, think I am done!"

"It's been over a year since Kate left. I know you must get lonely?"

"Sometimes, but I would rather live the rest of my life alone than look for another woman. I am fine most days. If it's meant to happen again it will, if not I will live."

"I never for a minute thought Kate would leave you the way she did. I am still shocked by it and I hate to bring it up but I really do hope you find someone special. We never know when our life can be flipped in a second. I always saw Brent as a good guy. That must have hurt you big time."

"It was tough but I was not surprised really. I felt something was up about a year after we married because I know that's when our marriage pretty much died. I did all I could and stuck by her when I wanted to leave. Yes it sure did hurt more that it was Brent. We knew each other a long time. We went to school together. I should have left long ago, it was my fault too. At least I have finally worked on fixing my own weaknesses. I'm no angel for sure. We were just not good together as a couple. Live and learn."

"What about that woman you told me about that you met a long time ago that you fell for, any word about her?"

"Melody is long gone. I went by her store a few months ago and the signs were all changed. Apparently she sold her shop and moved away. The new owners had no idea where, just that it was out of town."

"That's too bad my friend. I saw a spark in your eye when you told me about her."

"Yes, she woke something in me for sure. I hope she's well and happy wherever she is. I put her through a hard time back then because both times we connected I was married. I even lied to her the last time so she would talk to me, which was a bad thing to do to her. I didn't want to hurt my family by going through another divorce so it went nowhere unfortunately. If I had known what Kate was up to it would have changed things drastically for sure. Melody had warned me about Kate because she knew her from her own past. It was bad all around. I have many regrets about not being upfront with Melody from the beginning. She deserved better."

"Well, we never know what is around the corner. I do know you're a good guy despite your mistakes and you deserve to find happiness. I hope you find someone. The winters are long and cold here in Alberta. We all need some warmth."

"I agree with you there!" Wyatt stated as he brought the axe down hard and split the chunk of birch in half. He knew there would never be another woman for him like Melody and he kicked himself every day for not finding the courage to honour her the way she deserved, no matter how hard it would have been. He didn't lose his shirt the way he had feared he would either. Kate backed off once she was caught with his so called friend. Melody still came to him in his dreams some nights. He would wake up feeling the loss.

Chapter 24

FINAL GOODBYE

It was 3 am when Melody was startled awake by the ring from her phone. Her heart was racing when she picked it up and answered. Any call that came this time in the morning was not going to be a good one. She thought of her dad right away.

"Hello." she whispered holding her breath.

"Hello, is this Melody?" the lady's voice asked.

"Yes it is. Who is this?"

"This is Mary, your dad's friend. Your dad is terribly ill and is at the Bridgeport Hospital."

"OH NO!!" Melody put her hand to her mouth to stifle a cry!

"It seems he had a heart attack. He came knocking at my door, said he felt ill and collapsed right in front of me. I called the ambulance and they brought him here. The doctor is working on him now. Can you come?"

"I will be there within two hours. Thank you!" She hung up

from Mary and called Fiona right away. As soon as Fiona picked up the phone, Melody let out a sob. "It's my dad! I have to go see him right away! Can you call Eileen and come with me?"

"Yes, we'll be there in five minutes." Fiona said and hung up. Within five minutes she and Eileen were both standing inside Melody's doorway. They were still in their pyjamas. "We packed a few things in the car. We can change when we get there. We'll take my car. Are you ready Mel?" Fiona asked as she gave her a hug to comfort her.

"Yes, let's go! I so appreciate this. I just wouldn't be able to drive there myself." Melody said wiping the tears from her eyes as she rushed out the door to Fiona's car.

"You know we would do anything for you Mel, it's no problem luv." Fiona said as she opened the door for Melody to sit up front with her. Eileen jumped in the back. It was an hour and a half drive to Bridgeport and it was still dark. Getting them all there safely was Fiona's first priority. Eileen whispered a little prayer that Mel's dad would be okay and they would get there in time. Melody couldn't help but think of Wyatt and she wished he was with her to give her a hug. He gave the best hugs. She tried to push the pain in her heart away. Who would love her now if her dad died? It was too much for her to comprehend.

The streets were quiet when they pulled into Bridgeport. The hospital was lit up and easy to find. Fiona dropped Melody and Eileen off while she parked the car. They ran into the emergency room. When they got to the receptionist they were both out of breath. The receptionist looked up at them and said "Can I help you?" Melody took in a deep breath and said, "I am looking for my dad who was brought in a couple of hours ago. His name is Raymond Newman. My name is Melody Newman."

"Yes, take a seat." the receptionist replied. "Someone will be right with you. The doctor is with him."

"No, I won't take a seat. I want to see him now!" Melody demanded through her tears. She was becoming distraught and panicked. What if her father died before she could see him? She had begged God the whole way there to please keep him alive. He was the only immediate family she had left in the world and she didn't feel like being polite at the moment.

The receptionist picked up her phone and made a call. Within seconds a nurse came out and asked which one was Melody. "I am, where's my father?"

"Come with me."

They rushed down a hall and the nurse took her to a small room where a doctor was waiting. "Hello Melody, I am Doctor Carson."

"Where's my father??" she asked again. The panic was getting worse! Her chest felt tight!

"Before I take you to him I want you to be prepared. He is not well and is barely hanging on. He had a massive heart attack. I'm sorry to tell you he won't make it." Her legs went weak and she fell in the chair that was next to her!

"I need my friends with me. Can you please go get them?" she asked the nurse, now with a softer tone. Within minutes Fiona and Eileen were by her side and the doctor led them down the hall to see her dad who was in ICU...

When Melody saw him lying there hooked up to tubes and monitors her heart broke in two. She tried to stay strong but the silent tears fell. Eileen squeezed her hand before Melody took a step inside the room where her dad now lay lifeless.

Melody stood by his bed and took his hand that looked pale and tired. She noticed for the first time she was starting to get the same age spots on her hands that he had on the back of his. Those wonderfully, withered hands that did so much to show his love for her whenever she needed him her whole life. He had comforted her and wiped her tears away a thousand times whether she had scraped her knee or had her heart broken. He worked hard to always make sure their family had always been cared for with those hands.

Melody looked at his face and started having flashes of all they had been through together. All the good times and all they survived together, and now this. He deserved to die in peace knowing she would be okay. "Dad, can you hear me?" she whispered. She felt him barely squeeze her hand. "I love you Dad." He squeezed her hand again and he whispered something she couldn't understand but was certain in her heart that he said "I love you too." She kissed his face and whispered. "I know you do Dad. Don't worry about me, I'll be okay." She let out a sob no longer able to control the emotions she was feeling. "I'll see you again. Give Mom and sisters a hug from me and tell them I love them. It's okay to go with them now Dad." she whispered as she caressed his hands and face and kissed his cheek. There was just the slightest squeeze of his hand and he took a deep breath. Melody knew he was gone in that moment and that if she survived this loss she could survive anything. The pain in her chest was unbearable! She buried her face into his chest and sobbed.

Eileen gently grabbed Melody's arm before she collapsed and Fiona held the other one. They could see all the color had drained from her face. They both wrapped their arms around her to hold her up as they held her close and cried with her. "Thank you God for keeping him alive." she sobbed. She felt grateful for that much. "Give me a few minutes with him please." she said as she pulled away. The doctor rested his hand on her shoulder after checking her dad's vital signs. He said he was so sorry before he and the nurse stepped outside.

"Certainly luv." Fiona replied. "We'll be right outside the door when you need us. Take your time Mel."

Melody lay on the bed next to her father and wrapped her arm across his lifeless body to hold him and hug him one last time. It was strange that even at her age she suddenly felt orphaned. "How will I survive this?" she whispered in her father's ear.

Melody was grateful her two friends were with her. She would have been lost without them. They took her to a local restaurant after they had to coax her to leave her father's side. It was painful beyond belief and they knew she needed their help to do it. They were so patient and kind to her. She appreciated their love and support more than words could ever express. They helped her finish the paperwork at the hospital and helped her gather her father's things. They had cleaned up and changed their clothes in the washroom there.

"Please try and eat something." Eileen said. Melody just stared at the plate of eggs and fruit that sat in front of her. They could see that she was in shock. She only managed to sip some of the coffee that had now gone cold. It was hard for Melody to even swallow her heart hurt so much!

"We need to go to Dad's condo and take care of some things. He has a dog and I have to figure out what to do with her." Melody said in a whisper.

"No worries Mel, we can do that. Whatever you need." Fiona replied, squeezing her friends hand tenderly.

Chapter 25

MELODY TURNS FIFTY

Six months had passed since Melody had laid her dad to rest. She had struggled and fought her way back to some kind of normal. Heartbreak seemed to be a routine that she knew too well now. It was a strange feeling she couldn't explain being alone now in the world with no immediate family to talk to any more about all the memories of growing up. The pain of losing her father had been a real challenge to get past. As much as she loved her life and her friends, she felt completely alone now. Those moments she allowed herself to sit in self-pity, she felt abandoned. She never let herself stay there long because she knew it could become too comfortable and become an unhealthy habit. She missed her dad tremendously every day. So many wonderful memories were still fresh in her mind. He had given her so much great advice throughout her life. She often heard his laugh. He had the best laugh.

Melody brought her dad's golden retriever home to live with

her. Her father only got to enjoy her for a year and had loved her dearly. "She reminds me of you Mel, she's sweet and charming." he had said over the phone when he first brought her home. It had made Melody happy he was no longer alone. He called her Baby and Melody thought it suited her perfectly because she was so sweet. She slept on the rug near Melody's bed now and followed her around everywhere she went. Melody could see sadness in Baby's eyes too when she looked at her and sometimes coaxed her in bed with her when the loneliness of missing her father was too much to bear. Baby would snuggle into Melody's back. It gave both of them comfort.

Melody and her dad would take their guitars to the local pub sometimes when he would visit her. They always had a fun night and a friendly sing along with the locals who would bring their own instruments of choice. They would sit around a big table in the center of the pub and take turns singing old songs. Singing with her dad was something they both loved to do. He was a natural at singing harmony with her, something he had taught her as a child. It would not feel the same tonight without him being there for sure and Melody felt the dread in her heart but also felt the excitement of being with friends to celebrate her fiftieth birthday.

Melody knew her dad would want her to continue and live her best life and she was determined to do that, not only for him but for her as well. She took one last look in the mirror as she applied her soft, coral color lipstick. "Guess I am doing okay for an ole gal." she whispered. She was grateful to be fifty. She kept her hair just past her shoulders now and simply blow dried it, nothing fancy. She wore a knee length blue pencil skirt with a plain white t-shirt under her favourite jean jacket. She had a nice tan so she didn't mind showing her legs with her faded blue, slip-on sandals. "Casual and comfortable." she muttered under her breath. There was an ache in her heart that she knew would always be there. She saw it in her eyes every time she looked in a mirror. It seemed to have been there for many years now. The pain never left her completely of losing the people she loved the most in her life. Yet she functioned well despite it. She felt very strong in her will to live her best life despite her losses. Her family would want that for her.

Melody received many signs over the years from her mother and sisters that they were with her sometimes, and now from her dad as well. The energy was strong especially on the long nights when she sat alone with her guitar or while she sat quietly reading. Many times she felt someone gently touch her hair or her cheek. It always put a smile on her face. She knew in the deepest part of her heart they were watching over her. In those moments she didn't feel as alone. She had no fear of the unknown. Melody had learned enough in her lifetime so far to know there was much more to come after she would leave the earthly world and she believed in her heart it would be exciting and magical on the other side when she would one day join her family again. She was always curious about the afterlife and loved to read and learn as much as she could on the subject. She believed that God loves everyone, flaws and all. She believed that forgiveness comes from within. She loved having friendly debates on the topic and could usually get her opinion across without offending anyone. Her faith gave her great comfort through the tough times.

Melody told Baby to stay as she grabbed her keys and hurried out the door. She showed up at the pub at 8 pm sharp. Everyone greeted her with happy birthday greetings. They hugged her and made her feel loved. The pub owner Susie brought her a bottle of Chardonnay and a wine glass. "Happy Birthday Melody! This is on the house tonight." Melody hugged her tight.

"Thank you Susie and everyone for everything. I am sure feeling special."

Melody was happy to see Clyde with his dobra and Tommy was tuning his acoustic bass. Nina had her mandolin all ready to go and her friend Eileen had her violin. Grace, Jenny and Bridgette were there waiting with open arms too. Melody was so happy to see them all. Phil the psychic was there with his love. He lived not far up the shore from her. There were many hugs all around. They all gathered in their seats around the center table. There were some locals sitting at the bar and a few at other tables patiently waiting for the music to start. The atmosphere for a fun night was perfect and just what Melody needed.

"Thank you so much everyone. Not sure I will get a word out tonight because it's still tough for me with missing Dad but I will try my hardest to keep it together." she said in a shaky voice. "Cripes, I'm going to cry already." she chuckled and wiped a tear away.

Tommy called out as he raised his glass. "Here's to Ray, may he rest in peace! You are missed tonight Ray!" Everyone raised their glass and chimed in, "Rest in peace Ray!" Then he roared out again. "Happy Birthday to our Melody!" Everyone raised their glass again and bellowed, "Happy Birthday Melody!" Then they all sang Happy Birthday to her. She sat there smiling and taking it all in. Melody was glowing from all the love she felt. Tears welled up in her eyes knowing this would not be an easy night but a wonderful one filled with music and friends.

When she pulled herself together she picked up her guitar. "Thank you all. I want you all to sing this song that my dad and I sang so many times together. I know you all know the words and I will need your help, so don't be shy." she smiled. Melody heard the many murmurs of her friends support.

"We got ya Mel." Fiona stated with a big smile.

It sounded like the voices of angels singing at a distance as Wyatt lay down his head for the night. He knew there was a pub in the community. It had to be coming from there. He was staying at his friend's cabin for the weekend which was very close to the community of Acklin. He hummed along to the song knowing the words well. Will The Circle Be Unbroken was a song that brought warm memories of his mom singing.

Melody came to his thoughts and pulled at his heart strings as it did every night when he remembered her and longed for her. He suddenly felt warm all over, like someone had just laid a warm blanket to cover him as he drifted off to sleep.

Chapter 26

SURPRISE, SURPRISE

Melody woke up to a warm breeze blowing her curtains around. She forgot to close her window before she went to sleep and was glad she did. She lay there watching the curtains do their dance with the sunlight that peeked in the room. She could hear the waves from the lake gently rolling in on its shoreline. The leaves from the oak tree were rustling outside her window and the scent from her lilac tree filled her room. She felt lazy and didn't want to get up yet so she let her thoughts go to where they always did when she daydreamed, to Wyatt. For a long time after they stopped communicating she would push away the memories of him. It was too painful. Now she allowed herself to enjoy some of the sweet memories of him. The ache would always be there of missing him. She had accepted that a long time ago.

She closed her eyes and tried to focus on his face, his lips, his hair but mostly his eyes. She longed to see him again and have him look at her the way he did when she knew him. They had to have known each other in a past life, if there is any such thing. She believed there was because she definitely felt she knew him from some other time. She wondered where he was now and if he ever thought of her? Probably not… she was sure he was too busy with his wife to ever give her a second thought. She still struggled sometimes with the resentment but she was way better now than when she knew him. Whenever it bubbled up a little bit she would remind herself she had forgiven them both. She still remembered his scent to this day and if she let her mind go far enough she could remember vividly, every detail of his hugs and kisses. She was happy with these memories, ones she would never forget. Why would she ever want anyone else after such a beautiful connection that would stay in her heart and had filled her up enough for a life time?! His personality was very much like her sister Delia's, which made her feel even closer to him. They were sweet, kind and stubborn. Delia had been her best friend in the whole world too. She let her mind go back to how excited she always was to see Wyatt and how he made her feel like a school girl. She knew they were still connected, even though he was miles away.

"Okay, time to get up." she said as she stretched her body to get the kinks out. Baby jumped up from her slumber. It seemed they were both having a lazy day. When Melody pulled back the curtains the sun filled her bedroom. She had a sudden urge to go for a nice walk today. She slipped her feet into her cozy slippers that lay next to her bed, pulled her housecoat over her silk nightie and made her way to the kitchen to put coffee on with Baby strolling close behind her. Coffee would wake her up. After turning the coffee maker on she filled Baby's bowls with fresh food and water. "There you go girl." she said as she stroked Baby's fur.

When Melody pulled open the fridge door, there was the chocolate cake that was left over from last night staring her in the face. She grabbed the milk for her coffee and shut the door before she was tempted to actually have cake for breakfast. She was walking away and then spun around and pulled open the fridge door again. She reached in, took the container out and flipped the lid off. "What the heck, you only get to turn fifty once and I am going to enjoy it!" she muttered. She took a plate from the cupboard and cut a nice chunk off the cake and flopped it onto the plate. She turned on her radio, grabbed her coffee, cake and sunglasses and went out onto her deck to enjoy the beautiful day. There was a wonderful soft breeze coming off the lake and was perfect for relaxing. She took in a long deep breath of the fresh air.

Melody enjoyed every morsel of her cake that had a luscious buttercream, fudge icing covering it. It was just as tasty as it was the night before, if not better. She had opened her many unexpected presents at the party. She had told her friends she wanted nothing but their presence for her birthday. None of them listened. She felt very spoiled and grateful. She had shed some tears a few times during the night from her friends' kindness and from missing her dad but she had great support that got her through those moments. Eileen gave Melody a beautiful framed photo of her and her dad from one of the jams. It meant the world to Melody and she held it to her heart when she first saw it. "Thank you." she said as she gave her friend a huge hug.

A few times during the night Melody had to stop singing but the group didn't stop, they played on and let her get herself together and continue on when she was ready. It had been an emotional and amazing night!

Today I Started Loving You Again played on the radio in the distance as she closed her eyes and bathed in the warm rays of the sun. Her mind wondered right away to Wyatt. She remembered when he danced with her in her kitchen the night they shared a meal together. It was one of her favourite memories of him.

When she went back inside she took a long shower and brushed her hair and teeth. She pulled her hair into a ponytail, put on a simple, pale yellow sundress that fell to her ankles and she slipped on her white flip flops. She reached in her bathroom cabinet and took out the sunscreen and rubbed it on her face, neck and arms. "That should do." she said to Baby who was watching her patiently. Just a touch of lip gloss and she was done. On her way out she grabbed her white sun hat and sunglasses. A nice walk along the lake was something she loved to do often in the summer months. She carried her embroidered shoulder bag that had plenty of room to hold the latest book she was reading, a towel to sit on, some treats for Baby, a bottle of water and a few healthy snacks in case she got hungry. After that sweet breakfast she was determined not to eat any more sugar for the day. "C'mon Baby, let's go girl." she said. Baby was right beside her. Her tail was swinging back and forth excitedly as they walked out to the deck and onto the sandy beach.

They walked for a mile until Melody found the perfect spot for them to sit and relax. It was quiet on this part of the lake and she had a perfect view of the water. She could see fishermen further out in their boats. She enjoyed watching them pulling in their catch of the day. There was a wharf off to her right that the locals used sometimes.

Melody laid out her towel and sat down. She noticed there were two men just pulling up to the wharf in their boat. Baby sat next to her with her eyes already fixated on the boat. Melody pulled out her book and was about to open it when she noticed something familiar about one of the men. His height and physique looked familiar. He was wearing khaki shorts and a grey t-shirt with a loose fitting plaid shirt over it. It was his hair that caught her attention. She pulled off her sunglasses to get a better look. They were stepping out of the boat onto the dock. One man tied the boat to the dock while the other man carried a cooler, probably full of fish she imagined. She watched as he placed it in the back of a truck that was parked nearby. Melody suddenly felt anxious as she noticed the taller man looking her way. He was walking off the wharf and suddenly froze in his tracks and stared. "It can't be?!!" she gasped.

"Mel??" he called out.

"Oh my God, it can't be??!!" Her heart started beating fast!!

Wyatt walked towards her looking exactly the way she had remembered him. She would know his walk anywhere. He was still tall and lanky and his feet turned out a little as he walked.

She had always loved his walk. He had a little more grey in his hair but still beautiful. She couldn't speak! She just waved slightly as he walked towards her. She had goose bumps all over her body and she couldn't move! When he stood directly in front of her his shadow fell upon her. He reached down for her to take his hand and she did. When she stood her legs felt wobbly and she hung onto his arm to steady herself. When she looked into his eyes she saw tears in them. She knew his heart was racing too. "Puss." he whispered.

"Boots." she said with a look of disbelief in her eyes. It was like all the painful memories had disappeared and were forgotten at the very sight of him!

Melody held his face in her hands and said, "Look at us with our wrinkles now." They both laughed. The excitement of seeing him again was overwhelming!

"I can't believe it's you!" he said as he pulled her in for a long hug. She wrapped her arms around his neck and pulled him close to her body. She was shaking inside but was also smiling from ear to ear and was enjoying the feeling of being in his arms again. She pulled back so she could look at his face and touch him to make sure he was real. She put her hand on his cheek. They stared into each other's eyes with the same yearning they had so long ago. In that moment it was like nothing had changed.

Pain suddenly hit her heart that he could never be hers and she pulled away. She could see from the look in his eyes that Wyatt felt the switch from warmth to her being afraid. "I'm so happy to see you Wyatt. It's been a long time. How are you?"

"I'm great Mel. Better now. You look fantastic!" he exclaimed. "So this is where you went?"

"Yes, I needed the change. How's your wife?" she asked with some cynicism. She didn't want to waste any time. She wanted to get right to it. If he was still married she would escape quickly!

"Kate left a couple of years ago. She left me for my closest friend." Melody's mouth fell open. It took her a minute to speak again.

"Can't say I am too shocked that she did that. So you're divorced?"

"I am."

"Seeing anyone?"

"Nope!"

"Want to see anyone?"

"Yep, you?" he replied with a grin. The broadest smile came across Melody's face. The tears rolled down her cheeks as she hugged him so tight she thought she might break him in two! "Somebody pinch me!" she cried. Wyatt laughed and lifted her feet off the ground and swung her around. They were both deliriously happy! After he put Melody back down on her feet he took her by the hand and said, "I want you to meet my friend." They both walked towards Charlie and Wyatt did the introductions.

"It's so nice to finally meet you Melody. I have heard your name a few times." he grinned and looked at Wyatt. "Are you blushing?" he asked Wyatt. He was clearly getting a kick out of teasing him.

"It's so nice to meet you too." Melody chuckled as she shook his hand.

"Charlie has a cabin a little further down the lake. Go on without me Charlie, I will find my way back. I want to catch up with Mel if that's okay with her?"

"Yes, that would be great!" she replied enthusiastically.

"This is Baby by the way." Melody said patting Baby's head.

"Hello Baby. I didn't mean to ignore you." Wyatt said as he bent down to tousle her hair. Baby danced around with approval.

Chapter 27

WYATT'S PROMISE

The next morning Melody woke up to someone whispering, "Good morning Puss," in her ear. She had to let it sink in what had happened over the last 20 hours. Was she dreaming? Her heart was racing again. Is this for real? The man she had loved for years was now laying in her bed right next to her? She blinked to make sure she was awake. Yes, there was a warm body next to her, holding her, caressing her arm and now kissing the back of her neck. Happy tears trickled down her cheeks. She still couldn't believe that everything she ever dreamed of had suddenly come true. She never stopped believing that one day they would be together. If she couldn't have him she wanted no one else. And now here they were, wound tightly together.

Memories quickly floated back from the night before and she blushed at some of them. The love making was nonstop. They would take a break and start again. Neither wanted it to end! From the first all-consuming kisses on the beach, throughout their first official date together and all the way to the bedroom, was nothing short of electric! Wyatt had committed himself to her that night and only her. He looked at her and told her he loved her and there would never be another woman come between them. "I did the work Mel, you are safe with me now. I love you more than anything in the world." he had told her on their walk home. She finally felt she could believe every word he told her. She knew if she didn't she could ruin what they finally had together. She could see it in his eyes last night that he was being honest. He was laying it all out there for her to feel safe with him now. He had said he was sorry for all he put her through and he promised never to hurt her again. All the doubt she used to have was suddenly gone, just like that. "I believe you and I love you too." she had said to him and she kissed him deeply. Unless he gave her good reason not to, she would trust him completely.

She had forgiven him long ago for his lying and hurting her. Her faith in them, she believed in her heart, had brought them back together for good this time. She had always believed they were meant to be. "Just to be clear, if you do hurt me I'll have your head on a platter!" she had told him. His head went back with laughter. He had pulled her in closer and kissed her tenderly.

"You are welcome to do that but I'm not worried." he smiled.

Wyatt had kept his promise from years before. After Melody dropped Baby off at home and they went for a lovely meal, they sat on the beach and watched the stars together. This was the first date she had dreamed of having with him for so many years.

The skies couldn't have been more lit up and beautiful if they had planned it. By the time they got to her cottage there was no holding them back. They had both waited long enough to love each other in every way possible, and they did. He had captured her heart from the very beginning and now she felt certain she had captured his.

She turned over so she could face him and she pressed her face against his neck. She had the best sleep of her life in his arms. They both lay on their pillows with goofy smiles on their faces staring at each other. It was her favourite thing to do, to look at his face. Wyatt pulled her close and kissed her over and over. She was warming up again quickly. Melody took a breath and whispered, "We have to figure some things out later Boots." They had spent so much time kissing they had not talked a lot about expectations.

"Yes we will but for now I have other things on my mind," and he pulled her on top of him. She laughed and kissed him tenderly. All she heard was "Mmmmm."

Chapter 28

THE PORCH SWING

One year had passed since Melody and Wyatt had exchanged vows. It seemed like one month to Melody. They had nonstop fun and laughter together. The more they grew and learned about each other, the more they wanted to explore. The quiet nights of just lying in his arms was enough for Melody. She didn't need anything more to make her happy.

The cottage was everything they both needed or wanted. They were happy there. Wyatt had sold his home in Glendale within two months. He had pretty much moved in with Melody right away. He didn't mind the drive back and forth to work. He loved how comfortable and homey the cottage was and he especially loved the view. He said it was spectacular! The main thing he loved about it was she was there. Melody had told him it was his home too now and he could do whatever he needed to make it comfortable for him as well. Wyatt was building a garage right next to the cottage for all of his toys. He said he couldn't wait to take her ice fishing, and he did. Their adventures together were always fun and playful.

Wyatt loved Baby as much as she did him. She seemed to get a little jealous sometimes if she didn't get enough attention from him. She looked like she would actually pout. It was the sweetest thing to watch how silly she was around him.

Wyatt wanted to marry Melody right away and she was all in. Within three weeks after rekindling their love for each other, they were married. They had a small gathering on the beach in front of their cottage. Wyatt's family, their friends' and Melody's aunts and cousins made the long trip from the east coast to gather for a ceremony that made them both very happy. Wyatt had lost both parents, as did she, so they had framed photos of them placed on a table next to where they would exchange their vows. His children accepted and loved Melody. Wyatt was not surprised by this. Melody made sure Shelby and Matt were made comfortable in what was now their home too. They loved it at the lake and were going to stay there for the weekend while their dad and Melody went into town to stay at a fancy hotel to be spoiled. Melody and Wyatt didn't want to plan a honeymoon until later on when things slowed down.

They had picked out simple platinum matching bands that had their wedding date and each other's initials engraved on the inside of them in a heart. It was cheesy and sweet. Wyatt wanted to buy Melody an expensive diamond but she said no, she already had all she wanted in him. She didn't need anything flashy for him to prove his love to her. She felt it every day in the way he treated her.

Melody wore a simple dusty blue, A line dress with a lace bodice that showed a little cleavage for Wyatt. The dress was to the knee and flowed when she walked. Her grey eyes stood out even more with the blue shade she had chosen. She left her hair down in soft curls and carried a bouquet of white roses from her garden. Wyatt looked handsome in his white, open neck shirt and black pants. He wore a blue boutonniere on his shirt. They wanted the wedding to be elegant, simple and comfortable, and it was.

Wyatt was in his glee as he stood there waiting for her. Before she stepped outside the patio doors to the deck she called out to Wyatt. "Are you ready Jed?" Wyatt heard her loud and clear and he broke out with laughter. "Yes Granny, I'm ready!" he called back with a chuckle and a glint in his eyes. There were chuckles amongst the guests.

Melody looked down at Baby and asked, "Are you ready girl?" She had chosen her dad's trusted friend to walk her down the aisle. Melody wore a locket on her bracelet with two pictures in it, one of her parents and one of her with her sisters. She felt her family was right there with her and happy for her. She smiled from ear to ear and whispered to them, "I did it. I am happy!"

When she stepped outside on the deck and saw him standing there waiting, so darn sexy and sweet, she placed her hand over her heart and made the motion of sending it to him before she took the short walk out to the beach where he was waiting. Baby walked next to her like she had been trained to do. Melody felt like she was the luckiest woman in the world that day. Wyatt had a smile on his face and tears in his eyes watching her make her way to him. She was the most beautiful creature he had ever laid eyes on. Half way up to him she stopped and her band member Bobby handed Melody a microphone. The band played the music for an old Jim Reeves song called Welcome To My World. Melody started to sing the words and Wyatt was done! By the time she finished and got to him they were both crying. She took her lace handkerchief and wiped his tears first and then her own. When the vows were complete the minister said, "You may now kiss your bride." Wyatt leaned her back and landed a passionate kiss on his wife. The kiss went on and on and on... finally the minister said, "Okay, leave a little for later," and everyone broke out laughing.

Then the party started! They had a delicious catered dinner on their deck and they all watched in awe as the sun went down. It seemed to be more brilliant than ever on that special evening. Melody was sure it was the happiness in her heart that made it shine even brighter. There were many toasts and speeches wishing them well and the special words they had written for each other were heartfelt and brought the guests to tears.

Everything was set up perfectly for them and their guests to begin to dance the night away. Wyatt had a dance floor set up just off the deck. They had chosen the song I Can't Help Falling In Love With You, as their first dance. They had heard it playing on the radio and they both knew right away that was the one. "It's perfect Boots." Melody had said. They both had tears in their eyes listening to the words then, and it felt the same as they glided across the floor together on their wedding night. "I feel like I am floating." she whispered to Wyatt. He pulled her in tighter and sang along to the words in her ear. She loved his voice and knew how shy he was about singing which made it even more special to her. It melted her to the core. They ate, drank and danced the night away. It had been the happiest day of their lives!

On their first anniversary, Wyatt had given Melody a diamond heart shaped necklace with a two carat, flawless diamond right in the center of it. He knew she didn't like gaudy or clusters from listening to her talk about the jewelry business and her favourite things she had sold over the years. He had paid attention. They were always the simple, classic styles that she loved. It was beautiful and a nice surprise. "Wow, that is way more than I got for you Boots. Thank you!" she gleamed. She never needed or expected diamonds from him but it was beautiful and loved.

"You know I don't care about that. You deserve much more. Now don't throw these out the window Puss." he chuckled as he passed her a dozen pink roses. She cringed at the memory of her tossing the first one he gave her out the car window. That seemed so long ago now.

"I regret doing that. I wish I would have kept it." she frowned.

"I was lucky you didn't through me out the window, at high speed. I certainly deserved it." he chuckled. She held the roses in her arms and leaned in to smell them as he clasped the necklace on to her neck.

"Yes that's true." she laughed. "It's perfect babe. You know my taste." She smiled and kissed his cheek. "I just love it!"

Melody had asked for a porch swing as her first anniversary gift when Wyatt had asked her what she wanted. He told her the swing he had put together was for both of them so it didn't count. They spent every evening that the weather allowed from then on sitting on their deck in that swing watching the sun go down. Her gift to him was a new hunting jacket and a night of hot sex. She knew him well! When she walked in their bedroom that night wearing nothing but a smile and the jacket he seemed happy enough. "Yahoo!!" he howled. It was an anniversary night neither would forget.

Chapter 29

WHERE'S WYATT

Wyatt was off most weekends. Sometimes he would do a helicopter tour for a small group. He had taken Melody up for many rides already and as much as she was not a fan of flying, for some reason she felt safe with Wyatt. She pushed all her fears away when they flew around the hills and valleys near their home. She saw the beauty that surrounded them from a whole different view. "Wow, it is breathtaking Wyatt!" she exclaimed the first time he took her up.

Time flew by and was never boring for either of them. They went on two vacations together the first year they were married. The first one was to Newfoundland where Melody still had extended family. They spent a month travelling across the island visiting family and old friends. They stopped at many shops and bought some treasures and souvenirs for their cottage and for family and friends. Melody bought a beautiful homemade quilt for their bed.

The pastel colors were perfect for the cottage.

Six months after their wedding they had taken a vacation to Nashville. It was somewhere they had both dreamed of going and decided it would be their honeymoon trip that they kept putting off because they were so happy at home. They were both lovers of country music and had dreamed of one day seeing the Grand Ole Opry. It was a dream come true for them both when they finally went. It was a fantastic night of entertainment! They not only managed to hear and see many of their favourite artists but they got to meet one of them after the show. They had their photo taken with Vince Gill and had gotten his autograph. "I feel like I just died and went to heaven." Melody said afterwards.

"You're just in love with Vince." Wyatt grinned.

"I am." she said and smiled at him sweetly.

"I'm in love with him too." Wyatt chuckled.

Another big thrill was when Melody got to sing one of her original songs at the Bluebird Café. It was one of the many songs that she had now written for Wyatt. Wyatt sat back and never took his eyes of his woman as she sang. He wiped a tear away as he listened to the words of love she had written for him. Melody looked at him the whole time she sang it. "Damn, I'm the luckiest man alive!" he whispered.

Now they were home and all settled in for another winter. It was also hunting season. This was not Melody's favourite time of year because she would worry and miss Wyatt whenever he went off to the cabin with his friends. This time he was going to his friend Roger's cabin that was almost a two hour ski-doo ride away.

He told Melody he would be back in two days when he left. She hugged him long and hard and watched as he and Roger drove off on their ski-doos into the distance. Sometimes they had phone reception; sometimes there was none. It caused her concern but she trusted his experience and told herself he would be fine. It was something he loved to do with his friends and she accepted that. She wanted him to do his thing and for her to do hers with friends' sometimes. A little time apart never hurt them. It only made them stronger in their love for one another.

Melody planned on spending the weekend painting. She had not done a lot of artwork since Wyatt came back into her life because they had been so busy. That was something she would never complain about. Wyatt had told her he loved her paintings and she had promised him she would start again. He especially loved the one that hung over their bed. The first day he saw it he had said that the couple dancing in the painting looked familiar. She just grinned at him. "Do you like it?" she asked.

"I do. I think it's my favourite." he replied with a big smile.

She set up her easel near the big patio doors to catch as much light as possible and got started, not having a clue yet about what she would paint. She would just be in the moment and let the brush do the work in whatever inspired her.

She felt satisfied by the end of the day and smiled down at Baby and tousled her hair. "You made a good model sweet girl." She was pleased at how well she had done in bringing Baby's character into the painting. Baby had been sitting on a rug and looking up at her like she was patiently waiting for a treat. It was simple and turned out better than she expected.

The next morning she woke up with a feeling of fear in the pit of her stomach. She hated this feeling! Melody sent two texts and tried calling Wyatt several times. There was no response. She told herself he is fine but the feeling wouldn't leave her. She tried reading and knitting, anything to ease her mind but nothing worked. She couldn't focus. Baby sat by her feet and followed her around every time she moved to pace the floor. Melody knew Baby was sensing her anxiety. "He is okay girl." she said as she brushed her hand over her fur to calm her. Turning on the news to see a snow storm had moved in the area was not helping by any means. When she looked out her patio doors to the lake she could see drifts of snow swirl around as the wind picked up. The snow was coming down heavier by the minute. Her stomach was churning with worry.

Melody kept trying throughout the day to reach him with no luck. Finally at 2 pm her phone rang. She grabbed it and answered but it wasn't Wyatt, it was Roger. She sat down right away fearing the worst. She knew this would not be good! "Mel, it's Roger, we were out on our ski-doos and a snow storm set in. Somehow we got separated on the trails and I don't know where Wyatt is." All the blood drained from her body!! "Mel can you hear me?" Roger sounded as calm as could be. She cleared her throat and managed to get a whisper out. Her throat had gone completely dry.

"Yes, I hear you Roger. Bring him home!"

"I promise I will Mel, search and rescue will be out as soon as the storm settles. If we don't hear from him before then I don't want you to worry because you know Wyatt has all the skills to keep himself warm and safe. I am not calling his kids until I know more." She cleared her throat again and tried to speak up.

"Okay, keep me updated please!"

"I will Mel, try not to worry now." And the line went dead. The phone slid from Melody's hand to the floor. She lost all of her strength. "What do I do now?" she whispered holding the tears back. Eileen and Fiona were gone for the weekend to see friends in Glendale. She would only call them if she had to. She didn't want to disturb them. Melody left the TV on the weather channel and she paced the floor for the next ten hours constantly going to look out the window in case there might be a sign of Wyatt coming home on his ski-doo. She knew her world would end if anything happened to Wyatt! Her stomach hurt, her head hurt and her body hurt but nothing hurt as much as her heart! It was aching so badly, like someone was trying to pull it out of her chest! Baby looked worried too. Melody hugged her and rubbed her fur to try and reassure her. It was convincing herself she was struggling with.

"Please let him be okay Lord!" she prayed. When it became dark outside it only made things worse. She kept the tears inside because if she released them now she wouldn't be able to stop. So she kept her faith and made herself breathe deep and think positive as much as she could. She kept calling Wyatt's phone a hundred times with no luck. Sometime after midnight Melody fell asleep in Wyatt's leather chair with her quilt wrapped around her. She was exhausted! Baby lay at her feet and never left her side.

Chapter 30

GRIZZLY ADAMS

Wyatt was relieved that he found an empty cabin where he could hunker down and stay out of the storm for the night. He barely got out of the heavy snow that had fallen. It became hard to see more than a few feet in front of him and the sudden high winds didn't help the situation. Somehow he got separated from Roger on the trails. He hoped he was okay and made it back to his cabin safely. When it became hard to see Wyatt had pulled off the trail to the first cabin he came across. It was vacant and made do for the night. Wyatt hoped he could at least make a fire in the fireplace that looked pretty rickety and run down. He struck a match and lit some paper to get it going. Thankfully it worked. He placed a few more dried logs to it that were left piled up in a wooden box right next to the fireplace. He was counting his blessings! He opened a can of beans he had taken from his knapsack, along with a couple of Mel's biscuits and checked his phone. There were no bars left. Mel was going to kill him for sure. He knew how she worried. "Man, am I in for it!" he muttered.

Melody could hear Wyatt's voice calling out to her. "Mel, where are you?" She could see him at a distance through the fog but couldn't get to him. "I'm coming Boots!" she called, "I'm coming!" But as hard as she tried her legs wouldn't move. They felt like they were stuck knee deep in cement. When she looked down she had no legs. The shock of it woke her up! "Thank God!" she whispered realizing it was a dream. Her heart was racing! She wiped her hand over her brow to wipe the droplets of sweat away. Melody checked her phone. It was 5 am and not a word on Wyatt. She wished she could sleep until it was all over. Her anxiety was under control but barely. "Wyatt please call me." she whispered and then the flood of tears came. She couldn't hold it in any longer. She held her quilt close to her chest and let the tears fall. Her whole body shook from the thought of losing him again. It was better to release the tears. It only made it worse when she didn't. "This can't be happening!!!" she cried out. She pulled herself together and stopped crying as quickly as she started! "He is fine!" she said to Baby who was lying next to her and looked like she was about to cry too. She didn't want to give up hope or upset Baby more. "I am giving this to you God. It's too much for me to handle!!" she cried out. She felt a little relief right away.

She got herself together enough to take a quick shower. She fed Baby, made coffee and she forced a piece of toast and yogurt in her belly. She had been so hungry her stomach was growling. She checked on the weather and was grateful that at least the storm had finally passed. All she had to lean on was her faith, and she did. "He will come home soon Baby!" she stated firmly. Baby looked up at her as if she understood and agreed.

Two hours passed by and suddenly she heard a sound in the distance. She didn't move from Wyatt's chair. She put the TV on mute and listened. The sound was getting closer. Her heart was racing! It sounded like a ski-doo! She only got up to look when there was no doubt in her mind that was what she was hearing.

When Melody went to the patio doors and looked out she saw at a distance a ski-doo coming from further down the river's edge. She watched until it got closer. Pretty soon she could see the familiar details of the fur hat and the camouflage coat. "IT'S WYATT!!!" she yelled. Her arms flew up in the air and she danced around the living room!! Then she paced and waited, not wanting to look again in case it was a dream! "I'm going to fucking kill him!" she muttered. She held her breath as she waited and listened, and paced. Baby paced right by her side. Melody heard the ski- doo pull up to the cottage and she waited… she heard the crunching of the snow under his feet as he walked towards the door. She was still holding her breath. Melody pulled the door wide open and jumped in his arms! "BOOOTTS!!!" she cried. He wrapped his arms around her and held her tight. When he let her go she hauled off and hit him on his arm!! "You bastard!!" she yelled! "Puss, I'm sorry!! I know you were worried!"

"Don't fucking Puss me, why didn't you call?!!" she cried.

"I'm sorry Mel, my phone died! I was fine!"

"Oh, and like I knew that?!" she said now pacing the floor like a mad woman. "Come inside and close the door, I'm freezing!" she snapped. She had to calm down. He was safe!! Baby was dancing around and barking. Wyatt rubbed her down and said, "It's okay girl, everything is fine."

"When I was driving back I ran into Roger and a few men on the trail. Roger told me he called you. I just wanted to get back to you babe. That's all I cared about." With that she fell into his arms and wept like a baby. "I'm so sorry sweetheart." he repeated, kissing her head and rubbing her back. She was shaking in his arms. He held her until she calmed down and then she pulled away and swatted him on the arm again, more gently this time. He buckled over laughing. Wyatt picked her up and carried her to the bedroom. She was squirming and yelling at him to put her down. She couldn't help but break out laughing too. She was just so happy he was home! He gently tossed her on the bed. "You stay right there little lady." he said with a grin and headed for the shower. Melody lay there waiting anxiously for her Grizzly Adams.

Chapter 31

BIG DECISION

Wyatt and Melody had talked about having a child often. Melody didn't think it was possible for her to have one at the age of fifty two. They went to see their doctor and discussed options. The only way they agreed to try was to find someone younger who might carry a child for them. Wyatt feared there were too many risks for Melody. The doctor had told them after an ultrasound was performed that Melody still had a few eggs and they could try it and see what happens, but not to get their hopes up. It was called 'In vitro fertilization.' They would use Wyatt's sperm and her eggs to see if they would take, and if they did they would then implant the embryo into the gestational uterus of a surrogate. It sounded a little scary to Melody but she was willing to try.

"I would love for us to have a child together if it's what you want too?" Wyatt asked. It was something Melody never thought would happen in her life time. Since she had divorced Garrett, she had pretty much given up on it until Wyatt came back into her life. She had pushed it out of her mind because it was a painful thing she didn't want to think about. She loved children so much and had a way with them, and they loved her. She felt that Wyatt was the man she would want to be her child's father. Even though he had made mistakes in his past, he was a good man and had a big heart. She had watched and saw how much his other children adored him.

"I do want to try it Boots." Melody had seen a glimmer of hope after their last appointment.

"Okay, let's do it then!!" Wyatt was excited to give it a try. Melody laughed at his enthusiasm. She was getting a little excited at the thought of it too but also knew the reality that it might never work. She was afraid to get her hopes up too high. It was all very complicated but it was worth the risk that Melody was willing to take to become a mother and to have a child with Wyatt.

"Grace always told me if I wanted a child she would carry it for me. I will have to ask her to see what she says now. She is 42 now so she may not want to do it anymore. Her daughter is only two years old as well. It may be too much for her."

"All you can do is ask." Wyatt replied. Melody picked up her phone and pressed Grace's phone number.

"Hello doll." Grace said before Melody had a chance to say anything.

"Hi my friend. How are things? How is Maddy doing?"

"Things have never been better. She makes my world go round!"

Grace exclaimed. Melody could hear the joy in Grace's voice. She was so happy for her friend. She finally had found a good man and was settled in with him and her sweet girl.

"Can we meet for lunch later in the week if you are free?"

"Sure thing! Is everything okay Mel?"

"Yes, everything is fine. How about this Saturday at noon at the diner? Wyatt and I have to go into town to do some shopping and we could meet you then."

"Sounds great! I can't wait to see you both. Should I bring Maddy and Jack with me?"

"Of course, it would be great to see you all. See you then."

"See you then." Grace replied.

"It will work out Mel." Wyatt said as he leaned in and kissed her on the forehead.

"Let's hope so." Melody replied.

Chapter 32

AND THEN THERE WERE TWO

When Grace saw Melody she jumped up from her seat and reached out to hug her. They had not seen each other for two months and she had missed her friend. There were hugs all around. Melody leaned in to kiss Maddy on the cheek. "Hello beautiful girl." she said. Maddy lit up to see her Auntie Mel. Jack and Wyatt shook hands and they all sat at a cozy table in the corner of Ben's Diner. They chatted for a few minutes before the waitress came and took their orders.

When things settled down Melody reached across the table and placed her hand over Grace's. "I have a question to ask you and I want you to feel free to say no. I would understand completely."

"Sure Mel. What is it?" Grace had a look of concern on her face.

"I know it was a long time ago and everything in your life has changed now so my feelings won't be hurt if you say no. We are thinking of having a child but the risks are too high for me to carry one at my age."

"Say no more, done!" Melody looked over at Wyatt. They both looked shocked!

"That would be so cool." Jack said.

"You don't mind if she does this for us?" Melody asked him.

"Not at all. Grace already told me before she would want to do that for you if you ever wanted children. I told her I didn't have a problem with it."

"I am speechless." Melody whispered. Tears fell down her cheek. "And I'm grateful to have such wonderful friends." Grace squeezed Melody's hand and wiped tears from her own eyes.

"I am beyond excited to do this for you both! I don't plan on having any more, so it's just as well I do it for you. If I am meant to have a brother or sister for Maddy, it will happen when it's time. So just set up a time with the doctors and let me know what I need to do. I will see my doctor and make sure I am in good health first of course. I sure feel great."

"Well, that was easy." Wyatt laughed and then they all broke out laughing. Maddy started to giggle not knowing what in the world was going on. Just that all the big people were happy. It amazed Melody at how easily things came together since she and Wyatt were together. It was wonderful and she counted her blessings every day. Everything happened so fast nobody had time to question it. Within three months the procedures were all approved and Grace was already pregnant.

"I can't believe it!" Wyatt said when Melody hung up the phone.

"I know the doctor said it doesn't always work the first try.

Wow!! We're going to be parents. I am going to be a Mom! I'm so scared!" She was half laughing and crying.

"Too late to be scared now little Momma." Wyatt said as he hugged her. "Besides I do have some experience remember? We'll be just fine!" Both of them lay together lost in thought about how their lives would suddenly change. Melody let out a squeal of excitement and they both laughed! They were ecstatic!!

Wyatt and Melody were rushing to get to the doctor's appointment on time. When they arrived Grace and Jack were already in the room getting ready for the first ultrasound of their baby. They were all nervous and excited!

"Go on in, they are waiting for you." the receptionist said.

When they went inside the room Jack stood up to let Melody sit next to Grace who was already lying on the bed, prepped and ready. "Are you ready for this?" Grace asked them.

"As ready as we will ever be." Melody replied nervously and she squeezed Grace's hand.

They all stared at the monitor as Doctor Lacey slowly rolled the wand around Grace's belly. It didn't take long for her to pick up the heartbeat. "There it is." she smiled. They could see a little flicker on the monitor. Melody gasped! Tears were flowing and she kissed Grace's hand.

"Thank you." she whispered. Wyatt was in tears as was Grace and Jack.

"How exciting!!" Wyatt said. He had so much joy in his heart. He was beaming!

The doctor held up a finger to gesture to them to hold on.

"Can everyone be quiet for a moment please?"

"What's wrong?" Grace asked seeing fear in Melody's eyes too.

"I am picking up another heartbeat."

"What??" Melody asked, now in shock.

"Yes, there are two babies." Everyone went silent! They were all stunned by the news and held their breath!

"Just the two?" Grace finally asked hesitantly. She was getting really nervous there might be more. After a long pause and Doctor Lacey checking carefully she finally spoke.

"Yes, just the two." Everyone let out a sigh of relief.

"Thank God!" Melody said. Her first thought had been of Grace and how she would cope. "How are you feeling about this Grace?"

"I am good if you are?"

"I am just thrilled!!" Melody cried. "We won't have to do this again. Two children are perfect!" She said looking over at Wyatt.

"Yes perfect! This is fantastic!!!" Wyatt took Melody's hand and pulled her up off the seat. After hugging her tight he looked her in the eyes. "I couldn't be happier! We can do this together." he said.

"We sure can!" she exclaimed as she laughed through her tears. She was glowing! "I feel so blessed!" she said.

Wyatt leaned in and kissed Grace's cheek and said, "Thank you so much. You have changed our lives in a good way." He turned and vigorously shook Jack's hand and hugged him.

"Congratulations to you both! It will be fun being their Uncle." Jack said. They were all giddy with joy!

"It couldn't happen to two better people. I can do this with all your help." Grace smiled.

"We will be by your side the whole time and give you many breaks whenever you need it by taking care of Maddy. We will bring you anything you might need." Melody stated.

"As will I." Jack said, smiling from ear to ear.

"I am overwhelmed. It's our lucky day!" Melody said beaming.

"It looks like we need to make some room at the cottage, and soon!" Wyatt stated chuckling as he wiped a tear from his eye. "This is incredible. I know my kids will be thrilled as well!"

Chapter 33

COUNT THEIR BLESSINGS

Things had been busy at the cottage in getting ready for the twins. Wyatt had hired contractors to help build an extension with two added bedrooms and an extra bathroom. It turned out better than they expected. Melody was thrilled to decorate the nursery. She asked Grace to help her out in choosing the colors and furniture. She always asked Wyatt for his approval first before doing anything. He was fine with anything she chose. "I like your taste." he said.

Everything was finally finished and looked amazing. Wyatt added his own special touch in the nursery by adding two rocking horses that he had purchased and surprised Melody with. They were adorable and Melody loved them! She and Wyatt stood in the doorway and took it all in. It was a calming and peaceful nursery. "Grace helped me make decisions I was stuck on and you took care of the extension, so it was a group effort. I love the new space. It still feels like home. You would never know it was an extension. You and your team did a wonderful job Boots." She smiled as Wyatt leaned in for a tender kiss. "I am glad we stuck with the neutral colors until we find out what we're having. We can add more color if we want after they are home." she said. They had decided they didn't want to know the genders of the babies until they were born. There was two of everything. Two cribs, two cozy rockers, dressing tables and two dressers. There was a big area rug in the center of the room covering the hardwood that had soft pastel colors running through it that would work for a boy or girl. The closet and dressers were filled with everything and anything a baby would ever need. Fiona and Eileen had thrown a baby shower with all their family and friends invited who made sure anything they might need was covered. The bedrooms were big and as the babies grew they could eventually have their own rooms if they wanted. For now they would share this one. The shared bath was just as nice. All the finishes were done to suit the character of the cottage.

Grace was holding up well but was becoming anxious the bigger she became. Melody went into town at least twice a week to take Maddy out to give Grace a break. This was never a chore for Melody, she loved Maddy.

"Two more days!!" Grace squealed with excitement when Melody arrived at her door. They both laughed and hugged. "Come sit with me for a while, Maddy is still playing." she said. Melody took off her coat and followed behind Grace to the living area where they sat side by side on her comfy couch.

The time had flown by for Melody and Wyatt because they had stayed busy but Melody knew the last couple of months were hard and had gone by slowly for Grace. It was sinking in for them all what was about to happen. "My Mom is coming tomorrow and taking Maddy for the next few days until the babies come and to give me a little time to recuperate after. Maddy loves to go with her and grandpa. I will be ready and prepared when the time comes for these little troopers to make their great escape." Grace chuckled rubbing her expanded belly. Melody asked if she could touch her. "You know you can anytime." Melody smiled and reached over to gently place her hand on Grace's belly. Grace knew when Melody felt movement because her eyes would light up. Melody would always look at Grace and just shake her head, too choked up and overwhelmed to speak. "You are going to be the best mother Mel." Grace said covering her friends hand with her own. "I sure hope so Grace. I love them already."

Maddy ran into the room jumping in Melody's arms and hugging her. "You ready to go my girl?" Melody asked. Maddy shook her head yes and off they went. Melody took Maddy out to the local petting zoo and enjoyed the rest of the day listening to the view of the world through a child's eyes. She enjoyed every minute.

"Can you believe it?!" Wyatt asked Melody when he leaned in to kiss her goodnight.

"I know, I have butterflies!" she said as she pulled him in to kiss her more. "We have to take advantage of this time before we are officially parents." She giggled as she kissed him deeper.

"Mmmm, I'm in." he chuckled in a husky voice.

Melody never missed her chance to make love with Wyatt. There were nights she would wake up and become restless. If she just had the urge to snuggle and kiss his neck, that's all it would take for the love making to begin. They were matched very well in that department and neither ever turned the other one down. It was hot and constant and something she could never imagine changing no matter how old they would become.

It seemed like they had just gone to sleep and the phone rang and woke them up. Melody answered and listened while holding her breath. "It's time! We are on our way to the hospital!!" Jack's voice yelled sounding a little panicked.

"We're on our way!!" Melody yelled back and hung up. Wyatt was awake and up before she could even jump out of bed. They both showered quickly and dressed as fast as they could. They brushed their teeth and were on their way! They had a bag already packed for weeks now with things they might need. Wyatt grabbed it on their way out the door.

"My heart is racing!" Melody cried.

"Mine too babe!" Wyatt reached over to take Mel's hand as he drove.

When they arrived at the hospital and went to the delivery floor they saw Maddy sleeping in the arms of Grace's mother Brenda who had met them there. She said she was going to take Maddy to her place to sleep and they would come back in the morning. Melody had barely hugged them when she heard Jack's voice. "Wyatt, Mel, come this way!" Before they knew it they were all inside the room where poor Grace already was in excruciating pain. She had refused the epidural that was offered. She wanted to do this the natural way. Doctor Lacey was standing by and had checked Grace just before they got there. "She is dilated to 6 centimetres already." Jack whispered. "We were sleeping and she suddenly woke up with a sharp pain and that was it. Her water broke right after." He looked a little panicked and was pacing.

"Everything is okay now." Melody whispered and hugged him. "Go get coffee if you want."

"Yes, I think I will." he replied and left.

Grace cried out, "MEL!" as soon as she saw her and reached out her hand to her. Melody went to the bed and took Graces hand and gently hugged her. She would not leave her side now. Wyatt said hello to Grace and sat silently in a chair looking like he was about to pass out. Suddenly Grace cried out again and Wyatt got up to leave. The contractions were coming hard and fast. "I think I will go grab something to drink as well. Would either of you like anything?" he asked.

Melody said "Just bring coffee. That should be good thanks." Wyatt almost ran out of the room.

"Men are wimps!" Grace said, once the contraction wore off. It got her and Melody laughing so hard they had tears rolling down their cheeks. Jack came back to the room carrying coffee about twenty minutes later and Wyatt quietly crept in behind him. He passed a coffee to Melody. "Do you want your coffee sweetheart?" Jack asked Grace just as she was having a hard contraction.

"WHO WANTS COFFEE AT A TIME LIKE THIS?" she

yelled. Jack's eyes bulged and he backed into the corner and sat down not saying another word, slurping on his coffee. "I DON'T WANT TO HEAR ANY FUCKING SLURPING EITHER!!" Grace yelled again. Melody covered her mouth so Jack couldn't see her trying to stifle the laugh she was now holding in. It killed her to see Grace in such pain but like everything in her life, Melody saw humour in it too. Three hours of torture passed by slowly and Melody never left Grace's side for a second. With every contraction Melody would coach Grace to breathe the way they had learned in their Lamaze classes, but there were many moments when Grace would completely lose control. Melody felt deep guilt that she had asked Grace to do this for them with every pain her friend endured. "Don't worry Mel, it will be worth it and I will be just fine." Grace kept reassuring her. She could read Mel's body language. She knew her friend was feeling guilty.

Dr. Lacey came in the room and checked Grace again. "I think you're ready." she said. The two nurses gave the men and Melody gowns and masks to put on and then gathered around to help the doctor. Wyatt was still sitting with Jack in the corner of the room. Neither of them had hardly spoken a word. Melody motioned to Jack that he could sit with Grace if he wanted. He shook his head to indicate a firm NO. "The mothers should be together." he whispered to her, afraid he would set Grace off again. "Okay, thank you." she smiled back. The excitement and nervousness she felt was getting overwhelming! She held Grace's hand firmly and continued to wipe her forehead with a cool cloth.

"When you feel pressure then you can push down in your

bum Grace." Dr. Lacey said in a calming voice. And when the next contraction came Grace gripped Melody's hand tight and let out a yell that could wake up the dead!!

"There you go, excellent!" said the doctor. "The head is out. Hold on for a second and breathe." The doctor made sure the baby's head was turned properly. "The next contraction you can push down again Grace."

"NO FUCKING WORRIES ABOUT THAT!!!" Grace yelled at the top of her lungs! "Oh my, I didn't mean to yell at you, it's not your fault Doctor Lacey." she cried deliriously.

"No worries Grace, believe me, I have heard worse." the doctor replied. Melody could see she was smiling under her mask. "Breathe through it Grace, like you learned in class luv." Melody said.

"Yes I'm trying Mel! Is easier said than done!" Grace gasped and took a deep breath and bore down again. The next big grunt out slid a beautiful baby with a head full of dark hair. Melody released all of her anxieties at that moment and was now sobbing at the sight of her baby.

"It's a girl!" Dr. Lacey said.

"Is she okay??" Grace asked right away, waiting for the cry.

"She sure is." the doctor said giving her a tap on the bottom. Then the cry came. It was a sweet, strong and precious sound. The doctor let Melody cut the cord and passed the baby to the nurse. Wyatt was now standing right next to Melody and had his arm around her shoulder. "Okay, we are not done yet." the doctor said. "Ready for number two."

Grace let out a few more grunts and cries and out came baby

number two. "And it's a boy!" Doctor Lacey said with joy in her voice. "I never get tired of this!" she exclaimed. The doctor didn't have to pat this baby's bottom; he started to cry the second he was born. She asked Wyatt if he wanted to cut the cord this time and he did it with shaking hands and pride.

After Melody hugged Grace and they cried together for a few moments, she then stood up and wrapped her arms around Wyatt's neck and they held each other tight. They were all so relieved and happy!

The nurses weighed the babies and said they were both just over 6 pounds. They cleaned them and swaddled them in blankets and brought them to Grace. Grace shook her head no and indicated they were to be given to their parents to hold first. She had done her job, now she was the Auntie. The nurses gave the little girl to Wyatt to hold and the boy to Melody. Neither one of them could hardly speak a word as they held their precious babies. There was nothing but kisses and tears flowing. "They have your beautiful hair Wyatt." Melody said wiping her happy tears with a tissue.

"Thank God it's not grey." he chuckled and they all laughed. When the doctor finished taking care of Grace, Melody passed her the baby and put her arms around her. "How can we ever repay you?" she whispered in her friend's ear.

"Just seeing you both so happy is payment enough." Grace replied as she held her dearest friend and nephew close to her. Wyatt passed her his daughter as well in her other arm and gave her a gentle hug like he was afraid he would break her. He couldn't speak to say thank you, he was too choked up but nodded and smiled at her with tears in his eyes. "You're welcome." she said with a warm smile. Grace knew she had just accomplished a miracle for two people she loved very much. "This is a very fulfilling feeling to do this for two people I love, so the reward is huge for me as well."

Wyatt took something out of his pocket and handed it to her. When she carefully opened the small box it held a necklace with a pendant that held two heart diamonds in it. Inscribed on the back were the words, "Forever in our hearts, thank you twice." Grace was beaming! "Put it on me please." she said and Melody took it out of the box to do the honours. "Thank you both, I love it and will never take it off."

Jack caught all the tender moments on camera. "I'm proud of you Grace. Great job!" he said as he leaned in to kiss her.

"Even after me cursing you out?" she asked.

"Most definitely! I expected it. You were the same way when Maddy was born. It's all good luv." he chuckled.

"I'm sorry." she said as she kissed him on the cheek.

Wyatt took photos of Jack and Grace holding the babies too. The nurse came with a chart and asked what the baby's names were. Wyatt and Melody looked at each other and smiled. "You go ahead and tell them." Melody said.

"Anna Grace Walker and Wyatt Jackson Walker." Wyatt said proudly. Grace gasped and teared up touching her hand to her heart. "Awe, I love it! Thank you so much." she said beaming.

"Good names!" Jack said with pride.

Chapter 34

THE INTRUDER

So much had changed in their lives. Melody and Wyatt counted their blessings every day to be the proud parents of two sweet souls. There was never a dull moment in their home anymore. Wyatt had taken three months leave from work so he could help Melody with the babies and she was sure happy he did. They took turns feeding and changing the babies and many times Wyatt would do a double shift at night just to let Melody sleep. Sometimes they got up together if they weren't too tired. The joy they got from the little beings daily made everything worthwhile. Melody never knew she could feel this kind of love. There was no way to describe it, other than she would give her life for either of them. Of course she would do the same for Wyatt but this was a different kind of love.

Before long they were sleeping through the night, then crawling and now taking their first steps to walk. The entertainment from their giggles and becoming their own personalities was priceless. They would soon be one year old and time was flying by way too fast.

Melody was enjoying the peace surrounding her on a beautiful, bright and clear day. Wyatt had gone to town to pick up some supplies, the twins were taking a nap and she thought it was the perfect day to start a new painting. She set her easel out on the deck and set down the baby monitor on the table next to her in case one of the twins woke up. Today she decided to start a painting of her garden. The lighting was perfect for it.

She noticed an old pickup truck slowly driving by. The driver was looking her way and suddenly backed up and pulled into the driveway. The man rolled the window down and looked at her with a grin on his face. He looked in his mid to late twenties and was wearing a ball cap. He acted friendly but there was something about him that made Melody uneasy. "Good day miss, I was just wondering if you could point me in the direction of a good fishin' spot. I am new to the area and trying to find my way around here." He was smiling at her with his big chicklet teeth. There was one missing in front.

"If you go up the road about a mile that way, Melody pointed, there is a good spot right off the wharf."

"Okay, thank you miss. It's a mighty hot day, any chance I could get a glass of water if it's no trouble?" Melody felt her heart speeding up. "Stay cool!" she mumbled.

"Sure, I will grab you a drink from the fridge. I'll be right back." Melody turned and went inside, quickly closing the patio door behind her and locking it. Then she ran to the front door and locked it. The back door was already locked. Her hands were shaking as she tried calling Wyatt! There was no answer. She texted him one word. "HELP!" She ran to the babies room and saw they were still sleeping. She closed the door quietly. Suddenly she heard glass breaking! She ran to her bedroom to try and grab Wyatt's gun from the closet. She pulled boxes from the top shelf but she couldn't find it anywhere! When she tried to dial 911 the phone fell from her hand. "Fuck!" she whispered. It was too late, she could here feet running behind her and then something hit her in the back of the head!

When Melody came too she was dizzy. She tried focusing on what was going on around her. Everything was blurry. She didn't even know where she was at first. Then she saw a man rummaging through her dresser drawers and everything came back to her. She tried moving but he had tied her hands to the bed and put a cloth in her mouth so she couldn't scream. That was the last thing she wanted to do was scream and scare the babies. "Stay calm!" she murmured. She prayed he hadn't gone in their room or even knew they were there. She felt a sharp pain from the back of her head where he had hit her with something. He was going through her closet now. Thank God the gun wasn't there. Wyatt should have told her he moved it. The intruder was throwing things around and she could see he was putting things in a pillow case but she couldn't see what he was taking. The night table next to her bed had been opened and no doubt he had taken the extra cash that she kept there.

Her jewelry was locked away in the safe in the garage that Wyatt had put there for her, except for her necklace that she never took off. She prayed he didn't notice it. It was hidden well under the neckline of her t-shirt. Her wedding band she had taken off and was sitting on the easel where she had been painting. She always took it off before she used paints. It would be impossible for him to find the safe that was hidden away in the floor in the garage. They kept all their important papers there as well. Right now the most important things she cared about were her babies and their safety!

Melody stayed quiet but the minute he noticed she was awake he went to the bed. He kneeled over where she was lying and gave her an evil grin. "You know you're a pretty nice lookin' woman. I bet I could warm you up in no time." He chuckled in his croaky voice. Melody glared back into his dark eyes trying to show no fear! She had already decided that if he raped her she would stay silent and let him. She would do anything to protect her children! He was about to make a move when suddenly he stopped when he heard one of the twins crying. She could tell it was Anna's cry. "Who's that?" he asked, now seeming angered. Melody could no longer hide her fears! She started squirming to get away and tried to scream as he left her room. "NOOO!!" she tried screaming after him. Anna stopped crying! Melody was terrified and about to lose her mind completely!! She was nearly ripping her arms out of their sockets to try and get the scarf loose that he had tied around her wrist and then to the bed post. "NOOOO!!" she tried screaming again and again. She saw no way out of this!! "Please help us God!!" she pleaded with a muffled cry.

The man walked back into her room carrying Anna in his arms. He was smiling at her and talking to her in a playful way. Anna just looked confused by who this stranger was. She was staring at his face. Melody stayed as calm as she possibly could not to scare Anna. Inside she felt she would shake out of her body!

"You sit with your momma little girl while I check things out." he said and he carefully placed Anna next to Melody on the bed. Anna stared at her mother and Melody smiled at her through the tears that were rolling down her cheeks. "How nice that you have two babies lady." The burglar said as he left the room again. Anna looked confused and laid her head on Melody's stomach and stayed there. It was like she knew there was danger and wanted to stay close. It felt like minutes had gone by but it couldn't have been more than 20 seconds when suddenly there was a loud racket coming from the living room area. Melody heard things breaking and then a scream. Then Wyatt's voice filled the whole cottage. "WHO THE FUCK ARE YOU?? HOW DARE YOU COME INTO OUR HOME!!" he roared and Melody heard more things break!! "I GOT HIM WYATT, ENOUGH!!" another voice yelled out!

"MEL??" Wyatt called out as he went into the bedroom and saw her lying on the bed with Anna. "Are you alright baby??" he asked as he raced to her side. He removed the cloth from her mouth and untied her. He was shaking! "Did he hurt you Mel??"

"No, just a bump on my head. I don't know what he hit me with." she whimpered.

"Probably a hammer. There's one on the floor! Fuck!!"

Melody had never seen Wyatt look this angry or upset since she had known him. He saw the blood that had trickled down her neck as he checked the back of her head. "We got to get you checked out babe! I'll fucking kill him!!"

"No Wyatt, stay calm for the babies sake. I'm fine now." she said. He hugged her close and she wept. Her whole body was still shaking! Anna was playing with her fingers with a look of confusion on her face. She looked like she was about to cry too. Melody could hear baby Wyatt crying. "Go get the baby please. All the commotion woke him up. He's probably scared." Wyatt jumped up and went to the other room. Melody took Anna in her arms and soothed her. Wyatt came back holding their son safely in his arms. There was sudden relief for Melody that her family was all okay. She didn't know if she would ever get over this day. It was a nightmare!!

"Who is with you?" she asked.

"It's Officer Brinson and his partner. I called him right away when I saw your text. It scared the hell out of me! I was almost home. I thought they might get here before me but we got here at the same time. I tried calling you but there was no answer which made me freak out even more. Let's get your head checked out sweetie." He picked Anna up in his other arm, kissed her on the cheek and Melody held his arm as he carefully led them all out to the living area. Melody sat down on the couch and Wyatt sat the babies next to her. He got a clean cloth, filled it with ice and gently placed it over the bump on the back of Melody's head.

The cut was small but the bump was big. Melody cringed when he gently placed it on the bump. "You're going to need a couple of stitches." he said.

Officer Brinson asked if everyone was okay before they lead the now handcuffed prisoner out to their car. "Yes, I have to take Melody to get a bump checked but they are all okay. You can get her statement after the doctor checks her out if you like."

"Yes, we can do that." the officer agreed. "We will take a few pictures for evidence before we leave."

The guy had a swollen cheek where Wyatt had hit him. He was lucky the officers were with him because Wyatt wanted to rip his head off! The thought of someone harming his family was more than he could handle! He walked the officers outside but kept his distance now so he wasn't tempted to go after the guy again.

Melody looked up and saw Fiona and Eileen come rushing in. "Are you okay Mel?" Fiona asked when she saw her friend holding the cloth on her head.

"I'll be fine, just got a bump." she replied.

"My God, we were taking a walk and didn't know what was going on when we saw the police car pull in and then Wyatt pulled in like a maniac. We just saw the man they took out. Wyatt said it was okay for us to come in now. Did he hurt you anywhere else Mel?" Eileen asked hesitantly.

"No, I think he would have if Anna hadn't distracted him by crying." she said, holding her precious children close.

"We will take care of the babies and clean-up for you while Wyatt takes you to the doctor." Eileen said. Melody looked around the room, there were some things tipped over and broken. She didn't care about that. She was just relieved that they were all safe now. She knew the disarray was from where Wyatt grabbed the crook. The window in the back door would have to be replaced from where the guy had broken it to get in.

"Thank you, I will let Wyatt take me to the doctor. I am pretty sure the officers will want to take photos and collect evidence so don't touch anything for now."

Later that night when Melody and Wyatt were lying in bed, they shared their biggest fears from the day's events. Melody looked exhausted. The doctor had said she had a concussion and he had given her three stitches. He said that she should be fine and to just come back if she felt ill or light headed.

"I wanted to kill him! It's a good thing Brinson pulled me off him." Wyatt said still shook up from walking in his home to find the intruder heading to the kitchen. "He didn't see me coming from behind him." Wyatt had moved so fast and grabbed him; the guy didn't know what had hit him!

"Thank God you didn't kill him Wyatt. You could have gone to prison. I can't imagine that." Melody snuggled in closer. Wyatt had his long arms wrapped around her whole body. It made her feel safe. "I did my best to do the right thing. For once I didn't question what I felt. I could sense he was up to no good right away. I locked everything up as soon as I came inside. I wanted to choke him myself when he came in the room holding Anna in his arms!" The tears fell at the memory of seeing him holding her precious girl. "I wanted to claw his eyes out!" she said.

"You did everything right baby. He can't hurt anyone now." Wyatt whispered as he kissed her forehead.

"Where is the gun Wyatt? You didn't tell me you moved it."

"I'm sorry. I put it in the safe in the garage when the babies came home. I don't know why, I guess I took extra precautions. I should have told you but it slipped my mind at the time. You were out and I meant to tell you when you got home. I think now though, it might have been a good thing. Who knows what would have happened if either of you found it, you might have been hurt more, so it's all good."

"True." she replied. "I knew it was the only gun you kept in the house. There is no way I would have had a chance to go and get one of your hunting rifles in the garage. There just wasn't enough time."

"I am buying a solid oak door to put in the back tomorrow. No more doors with windows."

"Oh my word, don't go crazy now." Melody giggled as she snuggled into his arms and drifted off. Wyatt watched her sleep and pulled her in a little closer. He couldn't help but think of how badly this could have ended.

Chapter 35

FORGIVENESS

Officer Brinson and Officer Lucas showed up the next day and knocked on the new door that Wyatt had already installed. He took an extra precaution and had added a peep hole. Wyatt opened the door and welcomed them inside.

"Good morning. Nobody is getting in this door." Officer Lucas stated noticing the dead bolt Wyatt had installed on it as well.

"You young men want a coffee or something else to drink?" Wyatt asked as they stepped inside.

"No thank you Mr. Walker. We are just here to see how you are all doing and to fill you in on Bert Nevilles. That's the fellow's name that broke in here. Good morning Mrs. Walker," Officer Brinson said when Melody entered the room. She nodded her head and said hello to them. She waited to hear what information they had.

"So what's the story on the crook?" Wyatt asked impatiently.

He still wanted to knock the guy's head off!

"Not surprisingly the guy has a record a mile long. He has many charges of breaking and entering and had been charged with assault once before in a bar fight. I think this time he will be going away for a long time. Breaking into your home and assaulting your wife will put him away for many years." Officer Brinson stated.

"Good, I hope he never gets out!" Wyatt replied with venom in his voice.

Melody was standing by listening and didn't say anything at first. She didn't want to set Wyatt off any more than he already was but she knew her next comment just might do that. It was a risk she was willing to take.

"I want to see him." she said.

"What, why??" Wyatt asked her.

"I just want to see him."

"If you insist." Officer Brinson replied. "I don't know why you would want to? I guess if Mr. Walker is okay with it?" He turned to look at Wyatt for his approval.

"It's not up to him, it's up to me. I was the one attacked!" she stated firmly. She looked over at Wyatt warning him with her eyes.

Wyatt had no clue why she would ever want to see the crook again other than in court. That would be hard enough. He had to trust her in whatever her reasons were but that didn't mean he had to like it.

"We just need to make sure you don't try to go after him again if you go with her Mr. Walker?"

"No worries, I will restrain myself. She's definitely not going without me!" Wyatt stated firmly, grimacing at the thought of having to see the bastard up close again. It would be a challenge not to lose his cool but he would for Mel's sake. Melody nodded in agreement.

"Okay I will do my best to set something up for you."

Just one day after Bert Nevilles sentence of ten years, Wyatt and Melody walked into the local police station. Officer Brinson stayed with them as they were led to a room at the back of the station. The officer had said he would try his hardest to set something up before the prisoner was moved and he came through for them. They went inside a room and sat at a table. You could feel the tension in the room that held a strong scent of pine- sol. Shortly after another door unlocked and opened. There were two other officers that brought in the prisoner who was in hand cuffs. He sat to face Melody. Wyatt was sitting next to her on one side and Officer Brinson stood next to her on the other side.

A shiver went down Melody's spine. She looked the prisoner square in the eyes and asked, "Why did you break into our home and attack me?" He no longer had that smart aleck look on his face. When he opened his mouth to speak she cringed at the memory of him sitting on top of her smiling. He wasn't smiling now.

"I guess I am a fuck up!" He said in his croaky voice. Then he hung his head down. He paused for a moment and then spoke again. "To be honest I needed money. Things had been real rough after I got out of jail the last time and I had nowhere to go. I was sleepin' in my truck for weeks. I don't know what else to tell you other than I have bad addiction habits that I can't seem to break for long. I know that's no excuse. I shouldn't have tried to scare you either. That was stupid. I am a thief but not a rapist. What do you want from me?" he asked sharply. Melody could feel Wyatt's energy shift next to her but she refused to look at him. She knew he was pissed!

"Look at me." she said to the prisoner in a gentle but stern tone. He lifted his head to look her in the eyes. You could see he was as nervous as hell. "I would like for you to do better in your life. To take advantage of this time that you will be sitting in prison and learn the tools that will help you the next time you get out. You will still be a young man with your whole life ahead of you. I want you to forgive yourself for your past wrongdoings and to forgive the people that have hurt you in your past. That's what I want you to do!"

Wyatt was speechless! Melody wouldn't tell him why she wanted to talk to this person but he shouldn't have been surprised because he knew her heart. The prisoner looked shocked and now had tears rolling down his face.

"I'm so sorry I hurt you and your family." he whimpered.

"I forgive you." she replied and she gave Wyatt a nudge with her arm. He knew what it meant right away. It took him a minute to think about it and then Melody gave him a look.

"I forgive you too." Wyatt muttered just loud enough to hear. Bert nodded and mumbled a thank you, unable to hardly speak at this point.

Melody looked up at Officer Brinson. "We can go now." she said. "Good luck to you Mr. Nevilles."

The prisoner wiped the tears from his eyes and snot dripping from his nose with his sleeve. "Thank you." he replied.

As they were walking out of the station hand in hand Wyatt asked Melody why she felt compelled to do that. "Don't think for a minute it was for him completely Boots. I did it for us first. I don't want what he did to fill our family with fear and resentment for years to come. It had to be done to take back control of our lives. I feel much better now don't you?"

"Now that you mention it, I don't feel as angry anymore. It's weird."

"There you go! And I don't feel afraid of him now. He was born the same as all of us, with a good heart. Life messed him up. I'm just grateful things didn't turn out worse."

Wyatt took her by the arm and stopped her from taking another step. He looked in her eyes and said. "You amaze me Puss."

"I fucking amaze myself sometimes Boots!" she stated, and their heads went back as they both broke out laughing. "Seriously though, you know I am not overly religious but you also know I am spiritual and I do believe in God. I always ask myself, what God would want me to do in certain situations. Love and forgiveness are the two things that always come to mind right away. The hardest lesson to learn is to forgive ourselves when we mess up. I am not perfect and can curse and look how I struggled in forgiving myself for still loving you once I found out you were married. God knows our hearts though, who we really are inside and that's what will matter in the end Boots. He doesn't care if we mess up. That's how we learn to do better. He does care that we forgive and move on. Now if Nevilles would have hurt the babies I can't guarantee I could have done it so easily. Thankfully it didn't go that far. We have to be grateful for our blessings every day and we have many."

"We sure do. I love you Puss!" He put his arm around her shoulder as they continued to walk to their car.

Melody always made him think and see things in a different light. Through all the trials and tribulations they had been through, Wyatt was happy it was her that stuck by him and made the journey that much more interesting and worthwhile.

Chapter 36

GRADUATION DAY

For the most part, the years had been good to the Walker family. Besides the break in, things ran pretty smoothly in their home. Year after year the twins grew and became their own intriguing and beautiful people.

When Wyatt retired at 65 and the twins were 13, the family went on a vacation and spent the whole summer travelling throughout Europe. Wyatt's older children were always included in the adventures. It was always more fun if they joined them. They had also taken many helicopter adventures together back home. It was always fun and a learning experience for the whole family. There were picnics on top of mountains with incredible views. They loved enjoying life and spending family time together. The children had bonded Wyatt and Melody more, if that was even possible. They made them laugh hysterically at their constant quick wit and cry like babies if any of them were hurt or struggling.

Anna Grace was artistic and loved to dance. She looked like her mother in every way. Melody had put her in dance classes when she was three. She was a natural at it and was dancing and singing almost from the time she came out of the womb. She had been a cuddle baby, her brother not so much. He only liked to cuddle as a baby when he was sick. Wyatt Jackson was tall and lanky now like his father. He had the same beautiful head of hair as Wyatt Sr. only it was longer, dark and messy looking most days. It suited his character perfectly. Young Wyatt was a fisherman and loved aviation like his dad. Most times they simply called him Wy now. He liked it better around his school friends. Melody loved seeing him and his father bond in the things they had in common. Many times she would worry when they would go ice fishing together that there might be another storm but they always came home with big smiles and at least one or two walleye for dinner. She had never imagined there was a bond stronger than the one she felt with Wyatt but the children were the bonus of a love that was meant to be. Every day was another day of learning and enjoying each other.

Grace, Jack, Maddy and Jake were like family to the Walkers. Grace had given birth to their son the year after the twins were born. Giving birth to the twins gave Grace the desire to want to have another baby and a sibling for Maddy. They all gathered as often as they could for big family dinners and sometimes they all took trips together. Camping was the best fun! The twins loved their extended family and knew the story in how Auntie Grace had carried them in her belly for nine months. Many times they had listened attentively, wanting to hear the whole story again in how they came to be born.

It was when the twins received their degrees from university that Melody and Wyatt felt they could finally stop worrying about them, just a little. Anna Grace received a bachelor's degree in music and art, her goal was to teach and her brother graduated with a bachelor's degree in aircraft operations. His goal was to become a commercial pilot. Wyatt and Melody were proud and cheered loudly as each of them accepted their degrees. "They did good!" Wyatt beamed.

"They sure did!" Melody smiled. Her heart was filled with pride too!

That night the whole family and their friends had gathered at their cottage for a barbeque to celebrate. After they ate a wonderful meal of the best barbequed walleye, steaks and side dishes; there were speeches to send Anna and Wy best wishes. Melody gave a speech that turned into tears all around. She had talked about how she thought she would never have children, about how they turned out to be more than a miracle and had always made her most proud because they were good people. Wyatt stood up and simply said he was proud of his children and that Mel said it all for them. He was too shy and choked up to go on. They gave each of the kids a brand new car as graduation gifts. Although they were brought up fairly strict, as in not spoiling them too much, their parents had figured they deserved the cars because they had both worked so hard. Both the kids were shocked and overjoyed by their parent's generosity. Their parents made them work for everything and they would always get praise and pats on the back for being kind or doing a good job, but never material gifts, they only came at Christmas time or birthdays. This was a wonderful surprise and they were both ecstatic!

"I'll make you proud Mom and Dad." Wy said when he hugged them.

"You already do son." Wyatt replied as he gave him a tight squeeze.

"This is unbelievable!" Anna squealed as she hugged them both tight. "Thank you so much. I love it!" she said as she climbed in to look around her brand new cherry red car. Wy's was a cobalt blue color. Their parents made sure they were their favourite colors. They were perfect! Neither of them had known that the cars were hidden away in the garage for more than a week.

The fire pit was glowing on the beach and everyone had gathered around it enjoying the starry night and warm breeze off the lake. Wyatt passed Melody her guitar and said, "Sing me something babe."

"Not now Boots, I am enjoying myself relaxing."

"Please." She couldn't resist the look in his eyes.

"Okay just one, but   Anna, Wy, Shelby and Matt have to join in as well as anyone else who wants to sing along." Her friends from the pub had brought their instruments and Melody had been enjoying just listening to them play their own music. She had told them she just wanted to listen when they asked her to sing earlier in the night. "Which song should we do?" she asked.

"Can we do the John Denver song, Country Road?" Anna

asked. "I like that song."

"Good choice. Everyone knows that song." Melody stated. As they sang Wyatt stood by the fire and got lost in the sound of the voices. He loved to hear Melody sing more than anything and to now hear his children share in that talent made him beam with pride. His older children never seemed to take any interest in music but Melody had coaxed it out of them along the way. She even taught Shelby to play chords on guitar. Wyatt was in heaven right now listening to the beautiful sound with all the kids singing harmonies. Wyatt hummed along. He was the one person Melody couldn't coax to sing in front of people. She told him many times that he had a wonderful voice but he was just too shy. They had many gathering with their children where they had sing alongs and everyone would join in. Now to think Anna would teach music to others was a blessing all around.

Everyone clapped when they finished. Fiona yelled out "Sing a Patsy Cline song, Mel."

"Oh boy, I said one song."

"Just one pleeease." Fiona whined.

"Alright, just one. You started this." she said to Wyatt who was standing there grinning.

"Let me fill up your wine glass." he said. He grabbed the bottle from the tub of ice and bent down to fill her glass. "We should get a few more out of her now." he chuckled and everyone laughed with him.

"You're a brat!" she said with a grin.

Melody was feeling good for sure and she sang I Fall To Pieces like she never sang it before. If you could hear a pin drop on the beach you would have heard one that night. Nobody made a sound and the gentle waves rolling in seemed to be playing to the rhythm of the song right along with her. The whole night seemed magical!

To have a party like this was not the norm after a graduation. Usually most kids would just want to go with their friends. Melody and Wyatt were happy that their children wanted to share the night with family and close friends. Anna had even brought her new boyfriend, Tim, who seemed to fit in well. He and Wy seemed to have formed a bond already in loving to tease his sister. It was a wonderful night to remember.

Chapter 37

THE ULTIMATE HEARTBREAK

Christmas Eve the family was waiting for Wy to arrive before they sat down for dinner. He was driving from the city of Edmonton where he now lived and worked. Anna had arrived the day before with her now husband, Tim. Melody and Wyatt felt like they gained another son when Tim married their daughter four months before. Matt and Shelby and their significant others, Chelsea and Landon had already arrived with Matt and Chelsea's two sons, seven year old Braiden and six year old Branson. The boys were sitting quietly next to the Christmas tree building their Legos and munching on shortbread cookies. They were boisterous and sweet boys that looked like their dad. The adult children had all gathered around the fireplace enjoying taking turns playing cribbage with Wyatt. They loved nothing better than to beat their father and then rub it in. "One more game! Best two out of three!" Wyatt had repeated many times. It made Melody laugh every time she heard him protest when he lost. Matt was especially good at beating his father when it came to card games. Melody knew Wyatt loved the game, win or lose. It was the fun with his family he enjoyed the most.

Melody was in her element in preparing the meal. She would call on one of them when she needed a hand with anything. The kitchen was her domain and the kids loved it when she would ask one of them to do a chore, even if it was just to cut up vegetables or set the table.

Melody and Wyatt had gone all out in decorating the cottage and making it cozy and beautiful for their arrival. Wyatt had found and cut down the most majestic Christmas tree that was standing tall and lit up next to the fireplace. The pine fragrance filled the room. Christmas songs were playing quietly in the background on the stereo. Presents were wrapped and sitting underneath the tree. A few would be opened after the meal and the rest would wait until morning. Melody and Anna had spent the day before baking cookies. They had made enough shortbread for an army and Wyatt's favourites of course, chocolate dipped, coconut balls. Melody had got up early enough to add a black forest trifle and a raspberry cheesecake to the desserts. Wyatt had the fireplace glowing. It was heating the room and warmed the chill in the air from the cold wind blowing outside. They were all so excited to be spending this Christmas Eve together.

Melody was getting Wyatt to lift the turkey out of the oven for her to baste when she heard a whisper of Wy's voice in her head. It quietly said "Mom." That was it, nothing else. She suddenly felt panicked inside. "Something is wrong with Wy!" she said to Wyatt.

"What do you mean Mel?" Wyatt saw the sudden worry on her face.

"I just heard him call to me!"

"We just spoke to him five minutes ago. He said he would be here in an hour. He's fine!" Wyatt protested.

"Call his phone please!" She was trying to stay calm but her intuition had spoken and was telling her that something was wrong. So many times she would ignore it in the past but not today. Wyatt placed the turkey back in the oven and called his son's number. There was no answer.

"He is not going to answer if he is driving Mel." Wyatt stated, trying not to worry her more. He knew Melody's intuition was strong though and it gave him reason to take it seriously when she felt something was off. Anna walked in the kitchen and saw her mother's face.

"What's wrong Mom?"

"Nothing sweetheart. I am just a little worried that we can't get hold of your brother." she said, as she paced the floor. Melody's biggest fear in life was that she would outlive her children.

"He's fine Mom, he should be here soon." Anna said brushing it off.

Melody poured herself a glass of wine and sat in front of the fire where everyone was gathered. She sat in her favourite armchair and picked up her knitting that was sitting on the table next to it. She was finishing off a scarf she was knitting for Wy. He loved them and this was the third one she had made for him over the years. She wanted to finish it before he arrived so she could wrap it and give it to him in the morning. An hour and a half had passed and still nothing. Wyatt kept calling his number every ten minutes. Melody focused on trying not to worry but suddenly there it was, the knock on the door that she dreaded! Wy would never knock. He would walk right in to his home of 25 years like he always had. Always with a big smile and a smart aleck comment that would crack them up. Wyatt looked at Melody and put his hand out for her to stay seated when she went to stand up. "I'll get it darling." he said with all the care in the world in his voice. When he opened the door, sure enough there were two police officers standing there, the younger one had his head hung down. "Are you Wyatt Jackson Walker's Dad?" Melody heard one of them ask.

"Yes I am." Wyatt replied after hesitating, already knowing what was coming.

Melody could hear the voices but her brain was trying to block them out. All she could hear in her head was her inner voice screaming, NOOOOOOO!!

"I am sorry to inform you that your son was killed in an accident on the highway. He was hit by a snow plow that took a wrong turn." The world went black!

Chapter 38

PICKING UP THE PIECES

Four years had passed by since they had to lay their precious boy to rest. Wyatt and Melody would have died with him if they had a choice, but they had to go on and live their lives to the fullest not only for them but for the sake of Anna and for Wyatt's other children and their grandchildren who were also devastated by the loss. Anna had said she felt lost for a long time after her other half left. Having Wy as her twin was a bond no one else could understand.

The first night they got the news about their son, Wyatt thought he would lose Melody forever. She had fainted and Wyatt rushed to her side to pick her up to carry her to their bed. She was out for about five minutes before she came to again. As reality sunk in she had begged him for death. The pain was unbearable. Wyatt stayed by her side trying to get her to eat or drink anything in the days that followed. She refused everything in the beginning. Her screams were like the screams from a wounded animal that first night and for many days and nights after. It was earth shattering! When they lay together at night she would wake up whimpering and he would hold her and cry too. He had to keep his strength up to take care of her so he forced himself to eat and get up and get dressed every day.

Melody thought she knew grief but nothing came close to losing a child. It had ripped her soul apart! There were days she didn't know if she would make it. Melody kept dreaming of Wy. She had many dreams of him running along a beach and throwing a stick for Baby to fetch. When she would wake up she always felt Wy was at peace. Baby had passed when the twins were fifteen. They had grown up together and they were all heartbroken to lose her. Baby was laid to rest in their back yard. Anna and Wy had taken care of her burial plot under the oak tree. Melody would go to the back yard many times in the summer to hang sheets on the line and she would see that the kids had placed flowers there for Baby. It always made Melody tear up. She knew her dad would be pleased that Baby was loved so much. It gave her some comfort to dream about them all being together now.

After the first week of Melody pretty much living in bed, Wyatt told her she had to get up. She fought with him but he wouldn't let her oversleep anymore. "Okay, I'm getting up." she would whine when he wouldn't stop pestering her. Deep inside she knew he was trying to help her because he loved her and he was worried. Then one day after Wyatt had told her a dozen times, "Wy wouldn't want this," it was like something clicked on in her brain and she heard him for the first time. He was right! She had to keep going for Wy and for their family, but most of all for herself. She got out of bed, opened the drapes and stood in the warmth of the sunlight. She felt Wy was with her in that moment and it made her smile for the first time in what seemed like forever.

They got through the funeral somehow and decided to focus on the things they loved to do, now more than ever. The one thing Wy would hate is if they gave up on life because he had loved it so much. They would carry on for him but it was far from easy. At their age of seventy seven, it would have been easy to give up.

Wyatt would go off by himself hunting for days at a time. That's where he let most of his grief escape, not wanting to hurt Melody and Anna more than they already were hurting. He tried his best not to let them see him cry but there were times he couldn't control it. He was the rock for them when he was home and many times Melody cried in his arms for days. The grief would hit in waves for a long time after. "That's good, let it out baby." he would say to her and wipe his own silent tears from his face. Wyatt was her rock but looking at him sometimes made her heart ache even more. She found him many times wandering on the beach looking lost for weeks and months later. She would go to him, hug him and take his hand. They would walk together along the shore for as long as it took for the pain to ease up a little. Being close to nature seemed to help them. She knew he was being strong for her and the kids but his pain was easy to see in his eyes and his body language. He was a broken man inside for a very long time. The struggle was a real challenge but having each other's strength on their weakest days to hold on to, is what pulled them through.

Before long the cold days turned into the warmer days of summer. Weeks turned into months and then years. In time somehow they started to enjoy the little things in their life again. For many people a tragedy like losing a child tore them apart but for Wyatt and Melody they became closer and even more grateful for all the blessings they still had. They looked forward to what more would come with the other children and grandchildren and they still found joy in their little adventures together, but never without feeling there was a big part of them missing. The strength they found in each other only grew stronger in time. And then one day they laughed again. It was over some silly thing that Wyatt had messed up but it was funny and a relief that they could still enjoy each other's humour.

When the seasons allowed, Melody worked on her garden and she continued her artwork. She had not picked up her guitar since Wy left. Her heart would take a long time to heal before she could ever get a note out of what now felt like a big open wound. It still hurt too much! It was hard to wrap her head around the fact that he had died the same way as her mother and sisters did. It was crazy to her. How much was one person supposed to endure in a lifetime? Being a believer in God, she knew He had his reasons. She had her moments of great anger and questions for sure but her faith helped her get through every day. She would get her answers one day but in the meantime it still hurt, big time!

Tim was a rock for Anna when her brother passed. Melody worried about her constantly. "I promise I will call every day Mom." she had said to Melody when they left to go back to town just two weeks after the tragedy. Wyatt had often found Melody and Anna wrapped together sleeping after hours of crying together. It tore his heart out and he hated that he couldn't take their pain away. He was on the phone constantly checking in on his older kids that were devastated by the loss.

Wyatt looked Tim in the eyes before they left and said, "You take care of my girl!"

"I promise I will." Tim replied giving Wyatt a hug. Wyatt trusted he would. He had watched how caring he was to Anna.

Anna and Tim went on to have three children. They had one boy who was now three and the other two were twin girls who were two years old. They brought so much joy to their grandparents and they made life fun again. Melody could swear sometimes that Ryan was young Wyatt, reborn. He stuck to Melody and Wyatt like glue whenever they would visit. They especially loved when the grandkids got a little older and they could take them on little adventures along with Wyatt's other two grandsons. Wyatt especially loved teaching them all how to fish and swim, and diving off the dock was something they were always thrilled about. Melody would sit on the deck and take in the enjoyment of hearing them giggle and laugh at their crazy grandfather. Many times she joined in. Wyatt was always in his element and so patient and loving with them.

The twin girls Amelia and Abigail loved to learn gardening

and art. They also had an ear for music as did their brother. Melody had all the patience in the world in teaching them some basic lessons and they were naturals like their mom. The girls were lively, inquisitive and fun. Ryan was quieter and more philosophical. He had a dry wit that Melody enjoyed very much. She thought he might be a writer in the future. He loved to read and he listened intensely whenever they all sat around the fire and grandpa told one of his tales of his many hunting adventures with his friends. Some of it scared the girls but Ryan was always intrigued and wanted to hear more.

The grandchildren filled a deep hole in their hearts but the ache for Wy would never leave. His time was cut short but Melody had no doubt they would reunite with him one day and that was what kept her going. Wyatt's faith was not strong like hers but he did wonder sometimes if there was more to life after our bodies died. He sure hoped there was.

Chapter 39

MIDNIGHT SWIM

Wyatt passed Melody a glass of chardonnay and sat next to her on the porch swing that he had bought for their first anniversary. It was looking pretty rickety after thirty three years but still held up well after a few repairs. Wyatt often complained about it and wanted to buy a new one but Melody refused to give it up. She always said it was old and rickety like they were but still had a few miles left on it yet. "Cheers ole man." Melody said as she touched her glass to Wyatt's coffee mug. She still liked her drink of wine in the evenings but Wyatt had given up alcohol many years before. He said it was giving him an ulcer. Melody saw he was drinking a little too much after Wy died and that was why he had really given it up. He knew it might become a problem. He was a wise man and it was one of the things she admired about him the most, his common sense. She was proud of him.

"Cheers Puss." he replied. He put his arm around her shoulder and leaned in to kiss her forehead. She cuddled into his side.

It was a clear summer's night. The sun had gone down and you could see the full moon's reflection on the lake in all its glory. It made the lake look iridescent and magical. They sat there taking it in like they had so many nights together over the years. This was heaven on earth for them both.

"What do you think Wy is doing?" Melody asked.

"Probably flying a very cool helicopter." Wyatt chuckled. The thought made Melody smile.

"I bet he is." They turned to look into each other's eyes and each could see the sadness that never left their hearts from missing him.

"We've done okay sweetie." Wyatt said.

"We sure have babe." And she kissed his cheek. Melody loved these kinds of nights when they could relax and just talk about whatever came up. She loved how easy they always communicated. Many times they could read each other's minds without having to speak a word to each other.

"Our lives sure have turned out differently than I thought it might when we met all those years ago, especially after I found out you were married the second time. I could not imagine in my mind back then how we would pull it all together. It is amazing how everything changes when we find forgiveness in our hearts. It brings us the good stuff. I am happy I gave you another chance when we met again. I could have easily kicked you to the curb you know."

"Oh I know, you remind me all the time." he chuckled and gently squeezed her shoulder.

"I can't possibly imagine my life without you in it now. I knew from the first time we met we were destined to be together. I felt it right away. I have to admit though I wasn't sure if it would be here or on the other side. It wasn't looking good for many years." she said. "I can honestly say with my whole heart that I don't think I would have ever been with anyone else. I would be sitting here on this beautiful night staring at the heavens alone, sipping my wine and still wondering where you are."

"I can't imagine my life without you in it either Puss. With the exception of losing Wy, we have had the best years anyone could ever imagine. The other kids are doing well in their lives. You have been the best step- mom to my older kids. And you are still very hot by the way!" He winked and grinned. Melody smiled and pressed her face into his shoulder.

"I was so happy and surprised to run into Bert Nevilles and his family yesterday. I am thrilled that he now owns that flower shop. I would have never recognised him if he didn't recognise us first."

"It was because not only is he much older now but fixing his front tooth made all the difference in the world to his looks. He is doing so well and looks happy. He looks completely different. I thought he was going to shake my arm off when he came over and spoke to me." Wyatt chuckled. "I am happy for him too."

"Yes, he looks great and his wife seemed lovely. They have two grown teenagers together, imagine that? Just amazing! I almost felt proud of him in a strange way."

"Me too." Wyatt replied.

"Remember the night Boots, when I stripped all my clothes

off and you followed me, both of us naked as jay birds swimming in the lake under the moonlight?"

"How could I ever forget? It was chilly but things sure got heated fast." They both laughed as they relished in the memory.

"We should have done that more often." she smiled.

"Yes we should have but it got a little tough to do once the babies came."

"True." Melody shivered a little and Wyatt pulled her in closer to warm her. "I think we should give it a go now. Let's go skinny dipping!"

"Really?"

"Why not? We have to do everything we want while we are still breathing Boots. We aren't getting any younger you know."

"No kidding?" he laughed. "I'll beat you to it."

"Like hell!" Melody got up and walked ahead of him. When she got to the dock she pulled her dress off over her head and dropped her bra and panties on top of it. Wyatt dropped his t-shirt, shorts and underwear and climbed in right after she did. They were splashing around, laughing and squealing like two teenagers when they heard a car pull up. Melody hid behind Wyatt to try and hide the fact that they were naked. They saw two police officers walking towards the dock. They didn't get much traffic on the back road to their home but this was not their lucky night.

"Is that you Mr. Walker?" Officer Brinson asked as he shone his flashlight on him, then on Melody peeking from behind him, and then on the clothes that was laying at his feet.

"Hello Officer, nice night." Wyatt stated smiling nervously.

Melody felt her face burning as she smiled and gave a little wave. You could see from her expression she felt like she just got caught stealing candy from a candy store. She was blushing.

Officer Brinson shook his head in disbelief but was grinning from ear to ear the same time. "Well you folks be careful and have a good night."

"Thank you. We will." Wyatt said and put up his hand to wave as the officers turned to walk away. As they drove away Melody and Wyatt burst out laughing.

"We'll be the talk of the town now." Melody spurted out.

"Yep, not that I care." Wyatt chuckled. "Let's get out of here and take this to the shower." Wyatt said as he kissed Melody deeply. They still had it after all these years.

"I'm right behind ya Grandpa."

"That was fun Puss, thank you for suggesting it." he said as they quickly picked their clothes up and headed for the cottage.

"Anytime babe." she replied with a glint in her eyes. Melody patted his bottom as she walked next to him and took his hand.

Chapter 40

GOING HOME

Wyatt looked down at his Melody, lightly touching her hair and cheek. She looked as pretty as she did the first time he met her 50 years ago in her jewelry store. He put her through so much for the first fifteen years after they met but they had spent the last 35 years in bliss. He had never looked at or had any interest in another woman.

He kept his promise to her that she could pass on before him and she did, peacefully in her own bed at their cottage. He never wanted her to go through any more pain in her life. As painful as it was, he was glad she went first. It would have been too much for her heart if he left before her. It was he who had the heavy heart now and he knew it would stay that way until they met again. He felt certain they would. Melody had finally convinced him of that. They were both 85 years old when she went home.

She was the romantic one who believed in all that spiritual and corny stuff but truth be told he never doubted her intelligence. They had travelled together to many places over the years, had spent quality time together with family and friends. Her enthusiasm for life was infectious. He enjoyed her creative side and all the benefits that came from it. He grinned when some came to mind…

What he loved about her the most was her complexity. She could be sweet and elegant one minute and if he ticked her off, or when she was deliriously happy, she could take a swing at him and curse like a trucker. She was feisty and he loved it! She made him laugh constantly and when he was down or felt weary about anything, he knew he was always loved and cared for by her. She was everything he ever dreamed of all balled up into one amazing creature. He only hoped he made her feel as loved because she was more than worthy. He would miss her more than words could ever express.

He thought of all the cold winter nights over the years that they lay together by the fireplace as lovers or just talking and watching their favourite shows together. Their lovemaking was endless and the laughter they shared filled his life with so much unbounded joy. He loved her heart and how much she loved him and everyone else around her. She respected everything and everyone. She helped anyone who came in her path and needed it and most importantly even if they didn't, never expecting anything back. She loved making people smile if they were hurting, especially him. No other woman came close to how she could love. His hand went to his chest because his heart was hurting so much. He wiped the tears away and leaned in and kissed her forehead.

"See you soon Puss, I love you." he whispered. He could hear her voice in his head right away. "You better! I love you too Boots." He grinned from ear to ear and chuckled to himself. He could picture her laughing.

When Anna dropped him off at the cottage after the service she asked him if he wanted her to spend the night with him. "No baby girl, I'll be fine. I will call if I need you."

"Okay, make sure you do." she said with a look of concern on her face. "I love you Dad." She leaned in to kiss his cheek. She held back the tears being strong for him. Losing her mother was painful enough. She knew for her father it was devastating losing his soul mate. She knew he was holding up well for her sake too.

"I love you too." he replied and stepped out of the car.

The kids called out "Love you Grandpa." Tim chimed in and said "You take care Mr. Walker." Wyatt turned and waved to them all and called out "Love you too," before he disappeared inside the cottage.

The silence was overwhelming! Wyatt took off his hat and coat and hung them on the hooks near the entrance. He went to the kitchen and put the kettle on for a cup of coffee. No need to make a pot, it was just him now. He warmed up some moose pie from the freezer that Melody had made months before. He checked the date and mumbled, "Yep, should still be good." His mouth watered thinking of how tasty it would be. He turned the TV on to watch Dateline that he had recorded. It was one of his and Melody's favourite investigative shows that they had enjoyed watching together over the years.

After he ate and washed up the dishes Wyatt went to the bedroom and changed his clothes into his loungewear. He went to the bathroom and removed Melody's housecoat from the hook on the back of the door. He could smell her scent of lavender on it as he buried his face in it and held it to his chest. He lay on their bed and cuddled into the housecoat and the tears fell. He must have fallen asleep because he suddenly seemed to be dreaming. He could see her face as clear as day. She looked beautiful, like the first time he met her. She looked like she was glowing. She held out her hand and said, "Come home with me Boots." Wyatt didn't see her lips move yet he could hear her.

"But I am home Puss." he replied. She just kept smiling at him. Wyatt reached out and took her hand. Suddenly they were walking hand in hand along a beautiful beach. Wyatt stopped and grabbed her and swung her around like he did so many times over the years. It felt so real he was ecstatic!! She looked amazing wearing a soft pink, satin dress. Her hair was long and flowing down her back. There was a halo of daisies in her hair. "You look incredible Puss." he whispered, still not sure if this was real or a dream. When he looked down he could see from his hands he was a young man again. He was wearing a white linen shirt and pants. There was nothing on his feet, just some sparkles from the sand.

The water looked like gemstones that sparkled of emerald greens and blues, colors brighter than he had ever imagined. The sand looked like the softest color of gold and felt like silk underneath his feet.

In the distance he saw two figures walking towards them.

As they got closer Wyatt looked at Melody and asked, "Is that Wy and Baby??"

"Yes, it is!" she smiled broadly.

"How is that possible?" he asked, laughing from the excitement. He let go of Melody's hand and ran to them.

"Dad!!" Wy shouted as they hugged and clung to each other. Baby was jumping around them. Wyatt reached down and rubbed her head. Melody caught up to them and wrapped her arms around them. In the distance Wyatt saw more figures walking towards them and leading the way was his mother. They were all deliriously happy!

Wyatt looked at Melody and asked, "Am I dead Puss?"

"No Boots, you are very much alive. This is just the beginning." she replied and smiled.

After Anna couldn't get hold of her father all evening she and Tim took a drive to check on him. She already felt before she got there that her father had left to join her mother. It made sense to her. Neither could live without the other for long. This was how twin souls were meant to be. When they found him lying in bed and holding her mother's house coat it broke Anna's heart but she also had a sense of relief that her dad was now at peace. It would have been more heartbreaking to watch him wither away without her mother by his side.

After weeks had passed by Anna finally started the task she had been dreading, with the help of Tim and their children. They had to pack up her parents' cottage and put some personal things in storage for now. She had decided to keep the cottage for their family summer vacations. The children loved it there and Anna cherished the memories it held that were close to her heart. Her parents had told her she could do whatever suited her and her family. Tim was going to do some renovations first before they moved some things in that would make it more comfortable for them.

Anna was packing some things away in her mother's closet and looking through some boxes she had taken down from a shelf. They held many family keepsakes and some old photo albums that she leafed through. The photo's evoked many happy memories for her of her family and the tears fell. In the last box she found a manuscript. On the cover it was simply titled Dear One. As she leafed through the pages she could see that her mother had written a love story for her dad. It was their love story. The dedication simply said For Boots. Anna wept as she read some of her mother's words. It was filled with funny and heartfelt stories of their life together over the years. She would have to take it home to read it thoroughly.

On the first page her mother had left a note for Anna that said it was a life time of memories that she hoped she would enjoy reading and maybe try and get published for her one day after she had passed on. If it made any money she could do with it what she saw fit. "I never had the courage to let others read my writing." her mother had written. She had finished it just the year before she died by the date on the note. Anna remembered her mother had mentioned a long time ago that she had started a book. She had said back then she never thought she would finish it. And now here it was completed and left to her. Anna knew she had just found a treasure of memories that would never be stored away again. She had the book published in her mother's name and it went on to become a number one best seller that was then turned into a feature film. The proceeds went to her mother's favourite charity for feeding hungry children. The only thing Anna bought out of the money for her family as a keepsake and reminder of her parents love was a new porch swing to replace the old one. As hard as it was to take it down, it just wasn't safe anymore. Anna had the name of her mother's book Dear One engraved into the oak on the front of the swing. Anna knew her parents would love the way the cottage had been updated still keeping the character in it that her mother and father had loved so much.

"She did good Boots."

"She sure did Puss." Wyatt smiled.

ABOUT ME

I was born in 1956 in a beautiful, quiet town called Gander in the province of Newfoundland/Labrador, Canada. I lived there for four years with my family before my father accepted a job in Labrador. We moved to Happy Valley, Labrador for the next ten years and then moved back to Newfoundland to my mother's home, a little community called Clarke's Head, Gander Bay. My parents, Eric and Viola Waterman moved to Gander again in 1976 where they lived out there lives. I married a man from Labrador and moved to Fort McMurray, Alberta in 1978 following my two sisters who had already moved there with their husbands. I have resided in Alberta ever since.

I divorced my husband in 1998. I started to work in the jewelry business around that time. After working there for 15 years I decided I needed to slow down after being diagnosed with fibromyalgia in 2011. I had to quit the business. One year later, at the age of 55, I found my new love, writing. This is my third book since that time.

www.ingramcontent.com/pod-product-compliance
Lightning Source LLC
Chambersburg PA
CBHW021151110726
47900CB00002B/521